The AT4 had obliterated the door

Bolan flattened against the wall for an instant, then ran into
the opening, weapon ready. The room was a lobby,
detailed in wood and marble. It had a tile floor,
and was littered with the bodies of a dozen men. Blood pooled
around the blast area, and crimson streaks crossed the lines
on a road map, linking the fallen bodies and dropped
weaponry.

Bolan stepped inside.

The ceiling soared overhead, two stories high, with a
chandelier suspended from it. Bolan saw trace amounts of
blood on the lower rows of crystals, twenty feet above the
floor.

Not a living soul in sight.

That wouldn't last. By now Nuncio knew the building's
perimeter had been breached. Whoever was alive on the upper
floors would be beefing up their defenses. So far the soldier's
team was unscathed, but that was about to change.

From this point forward, the Executioner knew, blood would
be spilled on both sides.

MACK BOLAN ®
The Executioner

The Executioner
Don Pendleton's®

IVORY WAVE

A GOLD EAGLE BOOK FROM
WORLDWIDE®

TORONTO • NEW YORK • LONDON
AMSTERDAM • PARIS • SYDNEY • HAMBURG
STOCKHOLM • ATHENS • TOKYO • MILAN
MADRID • WARSAW • BUDAPEST • AUCKLAND

First edition June 2013

ISBN-13: 978-0-373-64415-5

Special thanks and acknowledgment to
Dylan Garrett for his contribution to this work.

IVORY WAVE

Printed in U.S.A.

There's no tragedy in life like the death of a child.
—Dwight D. Eisenhower

When a child dies, there is pain and heartache, but there's also the tragedy of a life unlived, of potential not being realized. There are far too many predators out there who just don't give a damn, who focus on the almighty dollar. My job is to thin the herd, to make sure justice is served.
—Mack Bolan

THE
MACK BOLAN
LEGEND

Nothing less than a war could have fashioned the destiny of the man called Mack Bolan. Bolan earned the Executioner title in the jungle hell of Vietnam.

But this soldier also wore another name—Sergeant Mercy. He was so tagged because of the compassion he showed to wounded comrades-in-arms and Vietnamese civilians.

Mack Bolan's second tour of duty ended prematurely when he was given emergency leave to return home and bury his family, victims of the Mob. Then he declared a one-man war against the Mafia.

He confronted the Families head-on from coast to coast, and soon a hope of victory began to appear. But Bolan had broken society's every rule. That same society started gunning for this elusive warrior—to no avail.

So Bolan was offered amnesty to work within the system against terrorism. This time, as an employee of Uncle Sam, Bolan became Colonel John Phoenix. With a command center at Stony Man Farm in Virginia, he and his new allies—Able Team and Phoenix Force—waged relentless war on a new adversary: the KGB.

But when his one true love, April Rose, died at the hands of the Soviet terror machine, Bolan severed all ties with Establishment authority.

Now, after a lengthy lone-wolf struggle and much soul-searching, the Executioner has agreed to enter an "arm's-length" alliance with his government once more, reserving the right to pursue personal missions in his Everlasting War.

Prologue

In prison, Dominic Chiarello had slept like a baby. He was protected behind the impersonal walls of concrete. His life was regimented—he knew his schedule, his routine. People he trusted surrounded him at mealtimes and in the yard. The first two men who moved against him had died quick but messy deaths. Word spread, and he was left alone.

Chiarello had enjoyed several perks: a plush job in the prison's law library, conjugal visits from his wife on a regular basis, his own TV, access to telephones and computers for emails, chats, and video conferences, and plenty of smokes and extra food. He had almost come to like it. Almost. But the constant reminder had remained that any fleeting sense of freedom he might feel was only an illusion. Deep down, he'd known that in spite of the perks, he was *not* free.

Because every night he'd gone to bed in a cage. He was safe, but so were the animals in a zoo, once the visitors were sent away and the gates locked.

Still, there was something to be said for certainty. Now he was out, and it had been twenty-five years and change, and the outside world, at least so far as he understood it, was anything but certain these days.

His nephew Massimo was waiting in a big black Escalade when Chiarello walked through the gates of the Ohio State Penitentiary in Youngstown one last time. Massimo had been a toddler when Chiarello went away; he had missed the boy's childhood, his high school graduation and everything else an uncle should be present for. Chiarello had sent gifts, and Massimo had visited him from time to time after he'd turned twelve. They knew each other. Not well—he had never once hugged the boy. But he knew his nephew, knew his accomplishments on behalf of the Family and he trusted the young man he had grown into. So when he saw him behind the wheel of the big SUV, he broke into a grin.

By the time he reached the vehicle, Massimo and another young man had emerged, and they opened both the front and rear passenger doors. Massimo came forward and enveloped his uncle in a burly hug. He had grown into a huge young man, well muscled, with dark curly hair and a broad face and lips that could entice women but then just as easily, Chiarello expected, turn cruel and dismissive. He smelled like cologne. Chiarello had once had a good nose for such things, but tastes had changed, new scents came along. Chiarello thought Massimo's was a little flowery, but maybe the women liked it.

"Welcome back, Uncle Dom," Massimo said as he held his uncle in a bear hug. "Glad to see you on the outside."

"Glad to be here," Chiarello replied. In most ways, he meant it. He tilted his head toward the other young man. "Him, I don't know."

"That's Brendan," Massimo said. "He's a good guy. You'll like him."

"Brendan?" Chiarello echoed. "He's not Sicilian."

"No. Irish, I think."

"Since when do we work with *them?*"

"Things are different since you went away, Uncle Dom."

"I don't like it."

"It's just how things are. It's about business relationships, about creating win-win scenarios. Not just about Family. Not anymore."

"So I've heard. I think it's bullshit."

"Times have changed, that's all. We still take care of each other. Trust me, Brendan has always had my back."

"If you say so."

"I do."

Massimo gave Brendan a nod, and the man joined them. He was skinnier than Chiarello's nephew, with a shock of reddish-brown hair that came to several peaks on top, like meringue on a pie. As he approached, Chiarello saw that he had a sprinkling of honest-to-God freckles across his upturned nose. Freckles! Chiarello glanced over his shoulder at the prison, wondering if they would take him back.

But only briefly. Outside the cage was still better than inside. Supposedly. Brendan came over and stuck out a hand, and Chiarello took it and squeezed. Brendan squeezed back. He was skinny, but strong. Chiarello gave a chuckle and released.

"It's good to meet you, sir," Brendan said. "You're like a, like a…"

"Yeah?"

"A legend, I was gonna say. Growin' up, we always heard stories about you."

"You make it sound like I'm already dead."

"Oh, no, Mr. Chiarello, that surely isn't what I meant at all. No sir. Not at all."

Spoken like a southern Ohio idiot. A hillbilly. Chiarello caught his nephew's eye, but the young man just offered a wan smile.

"We've got a long drive ahead of us," Massimo said. "We should hit the road. Uncle Dom, you want the front or the back? You pick."

"I'll take the back," Chiarello said. At least he could ride like a gentleman.

"I got shotgun," Brendan said. As if there was any other choice left to him, Chiarello thought.

Idiot.

ON THE RIDE, he dozed. He hadn't meant to, hadn't wanted to show any signs of weakness, of age or infirmity. On the inside, he had worked out sometimes. Not hard-core bodybuilding, like some of the younger cons, but enough to keep toned. For sixty-seven, he was in damn good shape. But when he woke up, as they were passing Cuyahoga Heights and crossing into Cleveland, he found a thin trail of spittle down his chin. The boys had been arguing about sports and women and cars, the way kids did, and he didn't know if either one of them had spared him so much as a sidelong glance since they'd left Youngstown.

The sun was almost down. He could see enough to tell that the skyline, while still recognizable, had changed enough in those years to be disorienting. "What the hell is that?" he asked.

"What?" Massimo asked him.

Chiarello pointed. "That monstrosity, there. That giant building."

"It's the Key Tower," Brendan said. "Tallest building in Ohio."

"It's bigger than the damn Terminal Tower. I love the Terminal Tower."

"That one in between them, that's the BP Building," Massimo said. "I guess they're new since you went away."

"I guess there's a lot of stuff new," Chiarello said. "I don't like it."

"The world changes, Uncle Dom."

"How's your father? He changed?"

Massimo chuckled. "He's the same old bastard."

"Well, that's one thing." Chiarello settled back into the

leather seat. He was awake now, and he wasn't going to drift off again. Anyway, they were almost there.

When Massimo turned onto the Inner Belt Freeway instead of getting off the highway and taking Superior west, Dominic was confused, but he didn't say anything. He didn't want to admit that he didn't know where the kid was taking him. Not to Vesuvius, the restaurant his brother Nuncio had owned for decades, where they used to gather in the front for Family occasions, and in the private room in back for business meetings. Instead, the SUV pulled into a garage beneath a modern, six-story office building on Rockwell. The structure was bland, with gray walls and very few windows. It looked more like a prison than the Ohio State Pen had. A gate rolled away as the vehicle approached, and as soon as they were inside it wheeled shut with a *clang*.

"Where the hell are we?" Chiarello finally asked.

"Headquarters," Massimo said.

"Here?"

"That's right. What'd you think, that Dad's pizza joint was still the nerve center?"

"Vesuvius is a fine restaurant. Upscale."

"Maybe once upon a time."

Chiarello was suddenly anxious in a way that he hadn't been since his first six months in prison. "You got anything for me?" he asked.

"Like what?"

"A piece! Something I can carry."

"You don't need anything in here," Massimo said. "We have state-of-the-art security. We're swept for bugs twice a day. Nobody gets through our defenses who doesn't belong."

"Still, I'd feel better."

"You can take mine," Brendan said. He drew a pistol from under his arm. Beretta, Chiarello noted. Probably Beretta U.S.A., but at least something around here was still of Italian descent besides him and his nephew. Chiarello felt its heft—a little light, but not too bad. He ejected the magazine, checked it and rammed it home again with a satisfying click. "It's .380 auto," Brendan said. "First round is double-action, and the rest are single-action. Eight-round magazine."

"Thanks," Chiarello said. "I'll give it back when I get my own."

"I got others," Brendan said. "So whenever is cool."

Chiarello was wearing a new suit, something Nuncio had bought for him and sent over. It was charcoal-gray with faint white-and-red pinstripes. He put the Beretta in his right jacket pocket, and its weight there comforted him.

The SUV stopped in a well-lit parking garage. Other high-end vehicles were scattered in the spaces. Massimo got out and opened Chiarello's door. "This way, Uncle Dom," he said. He led Chiarello to an elevator. Chiarello felt as if he was on his way to a dental appointment, or a meeting with a lawyer.

The elevator was clean, its brass polished, its lights bright. Massimo pressed the *L* button and the car rocketed skyward, smooth and silent. A moment later the doors whooshed open and Chiarello stepped out into a space that looked like a bank lobby with its teller cages ripped out. Across an expanse of marble floor was a curving reception counter with a brass sign on it that read NDC Consolidated Industries.

NDC. So Nuncio had put his own name first, even though Dominic was the older brother.

Chiarello patted his pocket, glad for the soothing weight at his side.

Things were going to change around here, he thought. He'd been away, but he was back, and by God things were going to change.

1

Mack Bolan waited for a clean kill shot.

As an experienced sniper, he was used to waiting. But he felt as if he had been doing nothing *but* waiting. Once he had identified and located his prey, he had waited to move against them—even though it meant leaving the young women to languish in captivity—because he wanted to learn how they planned to get their prisoners out of the country. Now he had found out. The men had loaded them into an RV and driven out into the Southern California desert, not far from the Arizona border. Bolan had parked a couple of miles away and hiked cross-country to the spot, then had had to wait in a cold spring drizzle at the edge of a remote airstrip. Finally an old Antonov An-72 cargo plane had landed on the strip, and as it taxied to a halt, the men had made most of their captives exit the RV first, then mingled with the last batch. Bolan couldn't take a shot without risking hitting one or more of the women.

They were girls, really, in their mid-teens to early twenties, and physically they ranged from pretty to sexy to stunning. They would command high prices on the human trafficking market. All of them were in the U.S. illegally, on expired visas, under false identification, or having crossed the border without documentation. One of them had done far, far worse than that. Their crimes, however, did not give others the right to victimize them. The men were Russians, and

Bolan expected their captives would be sold there, or in eastern Europe. *If* they were allowed to board that plane, which they wouldn't be.

He'd make sure of that.

The soldier was crouched behind a creosote bush, on a slight uphill slope, watching for his chance. He could see the men well enough to pick them out. Bobby McCrae, the dirty Immigration and Customs Enforcement agent who had identified the victims for the traffickers, had told Bolan—under considerable duress—what their names were and where they could be found. The taller one was Vasily, the blond one Andrei. Spotting the one female who didn't belong was harder. Bolan had seen her only once, in bad light, at a distance. She could have cut her hair, or colored it, since then. She blended in with the others, in terms of age and general appearance.

The only way she didn't blend was that they were victims of abduction, while she was a terrorist who had planted bombs at four sites around Los Angeles in the past two weeks. One had killed seven Americans, including four cops and two firefighters. The number would have been much worse, but by that time Bolan had been on to her, and he had been able to evacuate the embassy she had targeted. While the first bomb was being located and disabled, a second, smaller charge had gone off. As designed, it had taken out first responders who had come to the scene after Bolan had reported the original bomb.

Their deaths were on his conscience. He meant to make sure the women were taken into custody and deported, if need be, to their own countries, and to make sure the person known as Al-Borak—The Lightning—would never leave the country.

Bolan holstered his Desert Eagle long enough to take a couple of quick pictures of the airplane with his smartphone, in case he needed to identify it later. He was pocketing the phone and drawing the weapon again when one of the girls bolted. Another one cried out, pointing at the runaway as she ran for open desert.

The wait was over.

Vasily raised a 9 mm pistol toward the fleeing girl. Bolan didn't have a clean shot, but he had to chance shooting between two of the prisoners. His .50-caliber round didn't kill the Russian outright, but it tore off most of his lower jaw. By the time he slumped to the ground, blood was already spattering around him and mixing with the light rain.

Bolan charged toward the group, angling for a decent shot at Andrei. The Russian grabbed the youngest of the girls, an olive-skinned beauty with thick raven hair, and held her as a shield. Then Bolan saw another of the captives scoop up Vasily's pistol. This young woman had short frosted hair in blond and brown tones, and her lush figure was packed into a tight sweater and jeans that fit like a second skin. She could have been another victim, but her hard eyes gave her away. Bolan hesitated for a fraction of an instant, waiting to see where she pointed the gun.

When she sighted on the escapee, twenty yards away and still running, Bolan fired twice. The first round caught her center mass; the only effect of the second one—directly between those calculating eyes—was to make her die a little faster. He didn't think she deserved that small favor.

Andrei got off a shot that missed Bolan but hit one of the girls in the shoulder. They were all screaming now, and beginning to scatter. Their dispersal gave Bolan the opening he needed. He dived to the ground, dodging Andrei's second shot, and came up in a crouch. He snapped off another shot that caught the Russian in the knee. He spun around and collapsed, releasing his human shield at last. Bolan's next round blew brains and skull fragments all over the landing strip.

The cargo plane's pilot was standing on the pedal now, trying to gather enough speed to take off again without having to turn around on the strip. He wouldn't make it, Bolan knew—instead, he would plow into any of the girls who didn't get out of the way in time. The Executioner planted his feet shoulder-wide and aimed the Desert Eagle, supporting his gun hand with the other. He sighted carefully but quickly, and fired three times.

The airplane's windshield shattered and the pilot's head snapped backward. The plane's forward progress slowed, then it started to roll in a wide arc before coming to a full stop just beside the RV. Bolan could see just enough of the cockpit ceiling to know the pilot's blood had painted it red.

TWO HOURS LATER, having dropped off the RV and its contents at the nearest Imperial Valley sheriff's-office substation, Bolan made his second call of the day to Stony Man Farm. The sheriff had offered a department helicopter to get Bolan to the San Diego airport, where he could catch a flight home, and Bolan was just waiting for the bird to be fueled and ready to fly. He could use a little of downtime at Stony Man. He was still recovering from the physical trauma of a previous mission.

Hal Brognola answered on the second ring. "We've got a team on the way out to that landing strip, Striker. If there's any evidence on that aircraft that'll point to where it came from or what its destination was, they'll find it."

"They can pick up my rental car, too," Bolan suggested. "I left it parked a couple of miles away, just off the road. They'll be able to find it easily enough. And I want to know what they turn up—I'd like to pay a visit to whoever was going to meet those traffickers on the other end."

There was a pause that Bolan figured was Brognola taking his well-chewed, unlit cigar out of his mouth, and maybe picking off flecks of tobacco. "I'll keep you posted. In the meantime, you had a phone call routed here from someone named Gloria Fulton. Know her?"

At first the name didn't ring any bells. But Bolan racked his brain and came up with Eddie Fulton, a small-town Nebraska cop he had worked with once. Fulton had stumbled across a plot to blow up a railroad bridge over which nuclear materials were to be transported, and Bolan had gone in to help round up the perpetrators and ensure the train's safe passage. Fulton had known him under his Matt Cooper alias, but he had proved himself in so many ways that Bolan had eventually given him a phone number that would route to Stony Man in case any other terrorists showed up in the aftermath. He hadn't heard from the man since. But Bolan had met his wife once, during the case, and remembered a fiery-haired beauty in her early forties, with a ready smile and an infectious laugh.

"Yeah," he said at last. "Gloria Fulton. Did she leave a number?"

Brognola read it off to him. "Thanks," Bolan said. He could hear the stutter of the chopper's blades cutting the air. "I think my ride is about ready. I should be there sometime tonight."

"You did a lot of good, Striker," the big Fed said. "Tell you what, if you don't touch down until after 2300, take the night off. As far as we know, the world won't end before 0700."

"You've got another mission for me?" Bolan asked with a chuckle.

"Not really," he replied. "But I figured it might be a good time to come in and have a little more R and R. You got banged up pretty well last time out."

"I'll be in the War Room ten minutes after I land—and I'll expect to see you there. I'll fill you in on a few matters before I go off the clock."

He ended the call and glanced toward the helipad. The

chopper wasn't quite ready yet, so he dialed the number Gloria Fulton had left.

Five minutes later his plans had changed.

2

"To tell you the truth, Matt," Eddie Fulton said, referring to Matt Cooper alias, "I'm kind of embarrassed that Gloria called you. But I'm glad you're here, just the same."

"She didn't tell me much," Bolan said. "Just enough to get me here. I'm very sorry for your loss. Why don't you tell me what I can do to help."

Fulton's eyes filled, and he looked away. A father's grief was nothing to be ashamed of, but you couldn't tell a guy like Eddie Fulton that. He knew it already, but that didn't mean he was comfortable with showing emotional weakness to others. Especially to a man like Bolan. The fact that Bolan had known sorrow himself didn't help, either. Fulton was too close to it, on the verge of breakdown. Bolan had seen the signs before.

"Thanks," Fulton managed to reply. He wiped his sleeve over his eyes once, blinked back tears. "Damn it. I told myself I would keep my cool."

"Don't worry about it," Bolan said. "I know it hurts. Angela was a great kid. You miss her."

Angela was the Fultons' daughter. Thirteen when Bolan met her. A few weeks ago she had turned seventeen. She would never see eighteen.

When Bolan had reached Gloria on the phone the day be-

fore, her voice had been tight. He could tell she was fighting a
losing battle for control. "Angela's…she's gone," Gloria said.

"Gone?"

"She's dead, Matt. A drug overdose of some kind. Eddie's
just…I've never seen him so furious. I'm afraid he's going
to kill someone."

"Sounds like somebody deserves it," Bolan said.

"I guess you haven't heard. Last year he took a bullet while
stopping a jewelry-store robbery. It's near his spine. He's on
permanent disability. He walks with a cane, and not well even
with that. He's in a lot of pain, all the time. If he got involved
in something like—"

Her voice finally broke and Bolan could hear the sobs,
starting small but building fast. "I understand, Gloria. I'm
on my way. I don't know if I can get there tonight, but I'll see
you tomorrow for sure."

Now he sat in the Fultons' den in Makin, Nebraska. The
window shades were drawn and the house held a deep, for-
lorn silence. Gloria had greeted him at the door, then retired
to the kitchen. Eddie explained that their doctor had given
them some heavy-duty tranquilizers and they were both drag-
ging, barely functional. A bitter irony, considering Angela's
cause of death, Bolan thought, but he didn't say it.

Fulton sat in a big leather chair, with his cane propped
against it. He had put on weight, and his hair had gone almost completely gray. New lines around his eyes and mouth
spoke to the pain he had been through. He had a cup of coffee
on a little table next to the chair, and Bolan thought he could
smell the traces of something he had poured in to fortify it.
"I hope Gloria didn't get you here for nothing, Matt," he said.

"Tell me what happened and I'll be the judge of that."

"Far as I'm concerned, she was murdered."

"I thought it was an overdose."

"It was. And I'm sure she took the stuff of her own free

will. Since we saw you last, things have been…well, they've been tough. Especially on her. After I got shot, Gloria and Angela had the cop's family pleasure of waiting to see if I would die."

"But you didn't."

"No, but you know how it is for guys like us. Sometimes dying would be easier. I get to keep the title, but I'll never play the game the same. Anyway, Gloria was wrapped up and focused on my rehab. We were so busy that we barely noticed things had changed with Angela. By the time we knew she was into something it was really too late."

"What did she take?" Bolan asked.

"The stuff's called Ivory Wave."

Bolan had heard of it, but didn't know much about it. "Something like methamphetamines, right? Only they sell it as a salt or something."

"That's what they say. Except it gives a stronger, longer-lasting high, and can cause terrible hallucinations. Whatever happened made Angela slit her own throat. We'll never know why. And the thing is, they say this crap is perfectly legal. And it's deadly."

"It's legal?"

"It's sold as a bath salt," Fulton explained. "It's marked 'not for human consumption.' But they don't sell it in drugstores or bath and body shops—they sell it in head shops. Everybody there knows what it really is. It's poison."

"But if she took it voluntarily, knowing what—"

Fulton leaned forward. His face was turning red, anger boosting his blood pressure. "That's just it, Matt. She *didn't* know what the dangers are. There aren't any warning labels, there's no literature, no scientific studies. Because they can buy it in a store, kids think it's not as dangerous as meth. For that reason alone, it's more dangerous. Somebody cooked it up in a lab somewhere and slapped a label on it that got it around FDA regulations—they can add whatever shit they want. It's an open secret, but no one is paying it any attention, at any level of government. Kids are dying all over the world, but this…this is worse than anywhere. I've talked to cops in narcotics, Matt. This stuff isn't the same."

"What do you think is different?"

"I don't know, but I intend to find out. How can this happen? Right here…"

"In Makin," Bolan finished.

Fulton's fists were clenched so tight his knuckles had gone white. "If I had the bastard here who sold it to her, I'd—"

"That's just what Gloria's afraid of," Bolan said. "Not that she wouldn't support you a hundred percent. She just doesn't want to see you mixed up in any more violence."

"I can handle myself fine," Fulton argued.

"I'm sure you can. But she's already lost Angela. She doesn't want to take any chances with you. You're not going to think clearly on this one—that's why she called me."

"Yeah, I get that," Fulton admitted. He looked furious, but resigned.

Bolan was about to say something else, but Gloria called them for lunch. She had made sandwiches and iced tea, and as they ate, they tried to talk about other things. Every now and then the conversation circled around to Angela, then came to an uncomfortable halt.

After, Bolan left them alone and went to the motel he'd checked into late the night before. Makin was a small town, about an hour west of Lincoln on Interstate 80. He'd flown into Omaha and rented a car, driving through the calm, rural darkness. The town was surrounded by miles of farm fields and looked as flat as a concrete slab, and in town his lodging options were two motel chains. He had picked the one nearer the Fultons' home. It was no better or worse than the other, was about the same price and if the room had cockroaches, they probably weren't any bigger than at the other place.

Back in the room, he used his laptop to go online and search for Ivory Wave. The more he read, the angrier he became. People became addicted to Ivory Wave. It caused hallucinations, paranoia, suicidal thoughts, and drove up people's heart rates to dangerous levels. The rates of suicide in the region had increased sharply recently. Several law-enforcement officers around the country had been attacked, some even killed, by people under its influence. And as Eddie Fulton had said, it wasn't regulated because of the loophole that allowed it to be sold as long as it was marked Not for Human Consumption.

He ate dinner in the little coffee shop next to the motel, then went back to his room. Thoughts of Fulton's young daughter plagued his mind, but eventually he slept.

When he woke in the morning, before the sun, he was still angry. He took that as a sign. Something had to be done.

3

During breakfast, Bolan studied the contents of an envelope he had been given at the Fulton home. It contained photos of Angela, an annotated list of her friends and a couple of articles from local newspapers about her death. Looking over the material gave Bolan even more conviction than the night before.

He was no stranger to death. He had dealt it out many, many times, and had been touched by it in his own life. But he believed that it ought to mean something. Angela had been a good kid, an A student, interested in the world around her. She had planned to go to college, her folks said, and wanted to study microbiology, with hopes one day of helping to make headway against cancer. The past six months or so, she'd gone off track somewhere, but lots of kids did. Most of them had a chance to find their way again.

Not Angela.

When he had rescued them from human traffickers in California, Bolan had given more than a dozen young women a second chance at life. That felt good, but it didn't balance out the loss of the young woman he had known, someone whose parents he liked and respected. He was realist enough to know that taking out one drug dealer wouldn't make a difference to the world, but it would make a hell of a difference to Eddie and Gloria.

Eddie Fulton had told him that Angela wasn't the kind of girl who would ever set foot in a head shop. But that was where Ivory Wave could be found locally, so that was where Bolan would start. Already checking online he found that there was only one outlet in Makin itself, and the next closest was all the way in Lincoln. Since Makin's shopping district was small and mostly centered around River Road, he drove there and cruised until he spotted a place with peace signs and tie-dye and marijuana posters in the window. It was a small shop, tucked between a dry cleaner and a Chinese restaurant that didn't open until 11:30 a.m. The sign overhead said Flat Water Smokes-n-Stuff.

Inside, the place reeked of incense, and the woody smoke, combined with the black lights and grow lights and buzzing overhead fluorescents, stung Bolan's eyes. Almost every surface was crowded with merchandise or literature. The carpeting was mildew-stained and threadbare. A thin, goateed, thirtysomething white guy with light brown dreadlocks was standing behind a glass counter, on which he had what looked like an alternative newspaper spread out. He wore a tie-dye shirt that had probably come out of his own inventory, and through the glass case, filled with pipes and bongs, Bolan could see that his jeans had holes big enough to expose his hairy thighs. Two teenage girls were giggling as they approached him, one with a package in her hands. They were wearing clean clothes, and they looked like middle-class kids. Not unlike Angela, in other words. A bell tied to the door jingled, and they all looked Bolan's way, their eyes going wide.

He knew what they saw—a guy who was six-three, a couple hundred pounds of tightly coiled muscle, with short black hair and blue eyes that, he guessed, were blazing with urgency, striding in as if he owned the joint. He was wearing a navy blue windbreaker, a plain black T-shirt and blue jeans. He couldn't have looked more out of place.

Then he saw that the package the girl held was labeled Ivory Wave. He couldn't have said what changed on his face—maybe his mouth had turned down in a scowl or his eyes had visibly narrowed. But the girl, giggling just moments before, blanched and her knees started to quaver.

"You don't want that crap," Bolan said. He took two steps forward and lifted the package from her hands. "Forget you ever heard of it. And forget you ever heard of this hole, too."

Bolan crushed the package in his fist, then shook off the white powder that had gotten on it. The girls rushed out of the shop, and the proprietor blinked at Bolan, his mouth dropping open.

"You sell that poison to a lot of little girls?" the soldier asked.

"Dude," the guy said when he could compose himself, "you can't come in here and chase my customers away."

"I can't? I just did. If you missed it, I can do it again."

"What I mean is—"

Bolan didn't much care what he meant. "I asked you a question."

"I sell legal goods to people who are legally entitled to buy it."

Bolan showed him a recent picture of Angela Fulton. "How about her?"

The guy studied it. "She doesn't look familiar, but I can't say for sure."

"There anybody else who works here?"

The guy swallowed and glanced toward a doorway covered by a beaded curtain. "Jovan!" he called.

A moment later a second man pushed through the beads and joined the first behind the counter. Jovan was older than the goateed guy, and bigger. He was, in fact, a couple of inches taller than Bolan, and bright red curls added another inch or so to that. He was also a good hundred pounds heavier, much of it carried in a gut that preceded him into the room. But he looked solid, and he glowered at Bolan through a full orange beard.

"You think it's cool to scare our clientele?"

"I'm not much interested in what's cool," Bolan said. He showed the man Angela's photo. "Did you sell her any Ivory Wave?"

"I'm a businessman. What I sell to whom is no one's business. You got a warrant, let's see it."

"I'm not a cop."

"Didn't think so."

"You might wish I was, if you don't answer my question."

"What's that mean?"

Bolan had run out of patience. His right hand shot forward, grabbed the tuft of beard under Jovan's chin and yanked down. At the last instant he moved his right hand away and put his left on top of Jovan's head, pushing down into the mass of curls. Jovan bent forward at the waist—as much as he was able—and his chin smashed into the glass cabinet. The glass gave a loud cracking sound and fissures appeared the length and width of the pane.

When Bolan released him, Jovan straightened, touching his chin with one hand. His fingers came away bloody. "You cut me!" he said.

"You busted our glass case," his coworker added.

"I'm just getting warmed up," Bolan said. "The girl?"

"Dude," Jovan said to the goateed guy. "Call 911."

"Right." The skinny guy reached for a cordless phone standing in its station on the back counter. When he had it in his hand, Bolan reached over, grabbed a fistful of tie-dye and tugged the guy close, then took the phone from him. He threw it into a display of grow lights, where it landed with a satisfying crash.

"You ask me before you make any phone calls," Bolan said. "Understood?"

"Listen, man," Jovan said. He held his hands out, as if trying to appear compliant. "I don't know what's got you so worked up, but I'm sure there's a way we can settle this without anybody getting hurt."

"There is," Bolan agreed. "You answer my questions."

"That's cool."

"The girl," Bolan reminded him. Her picture was still resting on the cracked glass. This time Jovan looked at it closely. His hands were trembling, and a drop of blood dripped from his chin onto the glass.

"I don't think so," Jovan said.

"Be sure," Bolan told him.

While Jovan looked, the skinny guy eyed Bolan and then crouched behind the counter for a moment. He was picking up something that had fallen when Jovan's head met the glass case, Bolan thought.

But when he rose again, there was a shotgun in his hands. He pumped it once and pointed it at Bolan. His finger was on the trigger, and twitching.

"You know that's a mistake, right?"

"We have a right to protect our business," Jovan said.

As far as Bolan was concerned, they had forfeited those rights when they opened a business designed to profit from the drug trade. Pointing a gun at him only made it worse.

He sidestepped left as the goateed guy's finger squeezed the trigger. It might have been an accident, his nerves spasming his hand, but it didn't matter. The effect was the same. The weapon discharged, filling the narrow space with noise and smoke. The blast hit the painted brick wall across from him, tearing through merchandise.

Bolan caught the shotgun's barrel and snatched it from the guy's hands, meeting no resistance. Probably the first time he had ever fired a gun, the soldier thought. He kept the weapon moving in a tight arc and reversed direction, swinging the stock back into the guy's face, breaking the guy's nose with a gush of blood. Bolan ejected the remaining shells, then tossed the weapon onto the floor behind him.

By the time he was finished with that, Jovan had found a steel baseball bat and was charging around the counter. Bolan ducked the first swing, which whistled above his head. Jovan was strong, and the soldier knew he could do some damage if he connected. He dodged the second swing, then stepped inside the third and lashed out with a front kick that caught the big man just above his huge, swaying gut.

The air rushed out of Jovan and he started to double forward. Bolan met his chin with a powerful uppercut that snapped the man's head back. He followed with a left to his jaw and Jovan collapsed, gasping for breath.

Bolan knelt beside the big man on the floor. His face was turning purple, and his right leg was rattling against the floor. The left punch had dislocated his jaw, blocking his airway.

"This is going to hurt," Bolan said. Jovan's eyes glimmered with panic. He understood.

The soldier grasped Jovan's jaw with both thumbs and shifted it a little. The guy's eyes went wide and he gave a mewling sound, but his chest expanded and he sucked in a huge breath. Keeping his hands on his adversary's jaw, he made eye contact again. "Move from there and I'll dislocate it again," he said. "And leave it that way."

Jovan couldn't nod, but his eyelids fluttered. Good enough.

The guy with the bloody goatee was still on the floor behind the counter. He was unconscious, but breathing. Probably for the best—once he woke up, he would be hurting. Bolan left them where they were and passed through the beaded curtain into the back room, which had shelves full of merchandise, a neatly organized desk and a four-drawer filing cabinet. Bolan started there.

Jovan had said he was a businessman, and despite first impressions, he was apparently a careful one. At least, he maintained good records. It took a couple of minutes to find the invoice and packing slip for the most recent shipment that included Ivory Wave, but they were in the files. He pocketed them. Dry cleaning equipment could be noisy, but that shotgun blast would have alerted neighbors, and the police would be showing up soon, he knew.

He stepped back into the shop. The men were where he had left them. Bolan picked up Jovan's bat and spent a minute or so reliving his high school baseball days. He had been a power hitter, even then. When he was done, the shop looked as if a tornado had struck. Nothing made of glass was intact, and "bath salts," in their powder form, were spread all over the floor, mixed with shards of glass and plastic and dented, twisted metal. The only remaining intact bottle Bolan tucked into his pocket.

The last thing he did was pick up the photograph of Angela, which he slipped into his jacket pocket with the paperwork he had found. He dropped the bat into Jovan's lap. The big man hadn't budged. Blood ran from his nose and mouth in a steady stream and he breathed with a wheezing sound.

"I was never here," Bolan said. "And thanks for attacking me. You did me a favor." Again Jovan's eyes signaled comprehension.

Bolan was driving away when the first squad car skidded around the corner, lights going and siren wailing. He lifted two fingers in salute and kept going.

"HELLO, STRIKER," BROGNOLA said.

"Hal, I just wanted to let you know. That thing I said I was doing is going to take a little longer than I thought."

He had called Stony Man Farm the evening before, after meeting with Eddie Fulton. Hal Brognola understood that Mack Bolan set his own agenda, and their agreement allowed for that.

"No problem," Brognola said. "And listen, I talked to the President about that matter."

"About Ivory Wave?"

"That's right. He's aware of it, in general terms. But he didn't know how bad it had gotten out there. He said there are complications—his word—legislatively. The FDA would have to get the stuff classified as a drug before they could do anything. Congress can't seem to act. I don't know if the stuff has lobbyists, or what, but they haven't even managed to get a bill out of committee. For now, the President's hands are tied."

"Which is where I come in."

"More or less."

"I'm going to send you a sample of the local wares. I want to know how legal this stuff really is. I've heard of drugs doing some strange things before, but slitting your own throat is really hard core."

"That's easy enough. I'll get people on it right away to see what they can find out. These people are your friends, Striker. You do what you have to do. We can't get involved in any official way. But if you caused some trouble for the people making this crap and selling it, that would not be unpopular inside the White House."

"I've just started making trouble," Bolan said. "And I have a feeling I'll make a lot more before I'm done."

4

They met in the basement of Chiarello's house.

Nuncio had offered him an office in his downtown building, with sleek modern furniture and plush carpeting, even a lake view, but damned if Chiarello wanted to spend five minutes there. He hadn't spent twenty-five years in the can in order to come out and be a damn business drone, he thought. If that was the life he'd wanted, he could have gotten a straight job right off the bat, all those years ago.

Annamaria had complained, of course, when he'd told her the guys were coming over. "I was hoping we would have some time together," she had said. "You know, just us. To get reacquainted, before you jump right back into work."

She had gone completely gray while he was away, which was no surprise. She was still trim, but she had developed wrinkles and sags. Chiarello loved her, and he always would. She had never been the center of his life, though, and she wasn't now. "There'll be plenty of time," he told her. "The rest of our lives."

She had smiled at that. But she knew, as every made man's wife did, that there were never any guarantees. The rest of a guy's life could be decades, or it could be minutes. The key was to make sure you squeezed as much life as you could into whatever time you had.

That was why six men gathered in Chiarello's basement rec room, three days after he got back into town.

There was Chiarello. There was Artie D'Amato, who had been his lieutenant pretty much forever, and who had kept giving Chiarello his rightful share even during the prison years. Nico had been one of the guys at Ohio State who had watched Chiarello's back, until he was paroled three years ago and Chiarello had set him up with Artie. Dario and Ric were two of Artie's most trusted guys. And then, the biggest risk: Massimo.

But Chiarello had a feeling about Nuncio's eldest son. The kid had tried to act proud when he had taken Chiarello to the NDC offices, but Chiarello had sensed embarrassment behind the act. It wasn't surprising. Everybody knew who Chiarello was and what he had done, and it didn't take a genius to know he wasn't likely to be happy in some sort of corporate-type bureaucracy. Chiarello thought it was more than that, though. He got the impression that Massimo was an old-fashioned kid, with the right ideas about his place in the world. After all, when he was just a kid, his father had been in the Family business, too. It wasn't until after Chiarello had been gone for a while that Nuncio changed. Lost his nerve, his brother thought.

So he had invited Massimo to the meet, stressing that it was something Nuncio couldn't know about. It was taking a chance, but Massimo had agreed immediately.

Now they sat around Chiarello's poker table. The room was big and airy, with a wet bar, a giant plasma TV and a pool table. The walls were wood-paneled and the floor real Italian tile, put in by Annamaria's brother, who had trained in Milan. Massimo and Artie were smoking, and they all had bottled beer. Later on, Annamaria would bring in pasta and bread, if the meeting ran that long.

"You probably have an idea why we're here," Chiarello

began. "You all know I did a long jolt. I never named names, never said a word to anyone about any of our affairs."

"You always been stand-up, Dom," Artie said. "Nobody can take that away from you."

"Thanks. On the inside, Nico was my guy, my number one. He knows what it was like in there. Then when I hit the bricks, Massimo here was good enough to pick me up, bring me home. But first he takes me to this place, this fucking joke of an office building downtown. NDC Industries? What kind of shit is that? It's like Nuncio thinks he's fucking Donald Trump or whatever. A businessman. 'We're into all kinds of legit operations,' he tells me. 'The law can't touch us.'

"Yeah, well maybe they can't. But me, that's not what I signed up for. As a young man, I had a choice—we all did. We all know guys who took the straight road. You see them now and they look like they're already dead. Nuncio's earning, doing well, that's fine. But it's not just about the scratch, not to me. It's about the *life*. It's about the action. None of this bullshit about making drugs with bath salts—I mean, what the hell is that kind of crap." He turned to Massimo. "You're his son. I can tell you that it's not my intent to cause any injury to Nuncio—he's my kid brother, after all. But I do mean to shake things up. I'm going to push this Family back the way we were meant to be—the way we always were. If you don't want to be part of that, you better leave now. And if you breathe a word of it to your old man…" He left the threat unstated.

"I'm cool," Massimo said, meeting his gaze.

"Anybody else got a problem?" Chiarello asked.

Ric put his hands flat on the table. He had rings on every finger, and his black hair was long, combed back off his forehead, thick with grease. "Sorry, Dom," he said, "Nuncio's always been good to me. I can't go along with makin' any trouble for him."

Chiarello looked at Artie. "This how you run things?"

Artie shrugged, spreading his hands. In the organizational structure, he had come under Nuncio, while Dominic was away. He hadn't given up his other interests, the way Nuncio had, but there was an uneasy link between them, and apparently some of his guys remained loyal to Nunce. "He's his own man."

"Okay, Ric," Chiarello said. "You should probably go, then. No hard feelings."

Ric scraped his chair back and stood. "Yeah, okay. Nico, I'll wait in the car."

"Cool," Nico said.

"And you don't got to worry about me sayin' anything," Ric added.

"I know," Chiarello said.

When Ric started for the door, Chiarello caught Massimo's eye and jerked his head toward Ric. Massimo nodded. He rose and crossed the room fast, reaching the door right behind Ric. "Hey, bro," he said.

Ric started to turn. "Yeah?"

Massimo brought a knife out from somewhere. He moved fast, reaching one hand behind Ric's head, catching his long hair and jerking down to tilt his chin up. He slashed across Ric's exposed throat, then jumped back in time to dodge the first jet of blood from his carotid artery. It splattered wetly on the floor. Ric crumpled and went down, and the blood continued to flow until his heart stopped beating.

"Sorry about the mess," Massimo said. He crouched beside the now-still body and wiped the blade clean on Ric's clothes, then returned it to his ankle sheath. He returned to the table and took his seat.

"Don't worry about it," Chiarello said. "This tile cleans up easy." He went to Massimo's chair, took his nephew's head in his hands and kissed him on the forehead. "And that's good work," he added. "You're in."

MASSIMO HAD KILLED only once before.

That had been a different sort of thing, years before. He had been out with friends, drinking and generally carrying on. They had all been packing, of course, because everybody did then. Massimo had carried a cheap Davis P-32, a classic Saturday Night Special. After closing down a bar, they wandered down to the lakefront. One of them said something insulting to another similarly intoxicated group of young men. All these years later, Massimo couldn't even remember what had been said, or by whom. All he really remembered about that night was that he got mad enough to pull the little gun. He aimed it at one of the other guys and pulled the trigger three times. The reports seemed impossibly loud at the time, and it jerked around more than he had expected. Still, two of the rounds found their target and dropped the guy. They all scattered; Massimo didn't know until the next day's morning news that he had killed someone.

His father wouldn't have approved. He didn't like violence, he said, and he discouraged it in his Family and his "business associates." Massimo loved him, and he believed there was nothing more important than the bonds of family. His father, Nuncio, was only four years younger than his uncle Dominic, but Nuncio considered himself part of a new generation. Like his peers, he was moving into legit businesses, frowned on violence and generally tried to put the old ways behind him.

Uncle Dom, though, he was old school. He was a hard man, afraid of nothing that Massimo could see, willing to do whatever it took.

Massimo loved his father, but he respected his uncle. So when it came time to choose between them—not as a parent but as a leader—he had to choose his uncle.

Besides, he thought in the car, heading home to Carla after dumping Ric's body, this time he had liked it.

He had been carrying the Ka-Bar knife for more than a year, keeping it from his father the whole time. Some mornings, strapping the sheath around his ankle, he wondered why. "Just in case" got old, when that case never happened. The sheath sometimes chafed his leg, and he was sure there wasn't as much hair on that ankle as on the other anymore.

But he had seen an opportunity, this day, to impress his uncle. Besides, the old man had given him the high sign. Ric couldn't be allowed to leave. He would have gone straight to Nuncio and ratted them all out. Somebody had to take care of him, and his uncle had picked him. Crossing the room behind Ric, Massimo had felt a strange mix of anxiety, pride and arousal that bordered on sexual. The knife felt comfortable in his hand, natural. Then the attack itself, blindingly fast. The keen blade had parted flesh like hot steel through butter. It seemed to catch for an instant on the cartilage of the larynx, but then it sliced through.

He'd had to move fast to avoid that first arterial spurt. Some of it got on his clothes, which meant he would have to burn them. It was just a tracksuit, nothing too expensive, but Carla would wonder what had happened to it.

That was okay, he guessed. She had learned at an early age not to ask too many questions about his business, and even through the NDC years she had held fast to that tradition. Then, Massimo hadn't talked about work because it was boring. Now things were changing, and he wouldn't talk about business because a man just didn't.

The most important thing was the way it made him feel. Watching a man bleed out and die, thanks to something he had done, filled him with power. He was alive, he was male, he was a victor in life's most elemental battle. He would show Carla a good time when he got home, that was for sure.

And already he was looking forward to the next time. The next death.

Having done it once, in an up-close, hands-on way, he wanted more.

Maybe he was addicted. If so…bring it on.

5

Bolan was sitting in an empty classroom at Makin High when the door opened. The school's principal, Mr. Robert Vahle, entered, followed by a student wearing a snug black sweater and jeans with zippers all over them. She had a blue streak in her shoulder-length blond hair, but otherwise she looked like an all-American girl. "This is Tracy Hawkins, Marshal Cooper," Vahle said. "Tracy, the marshal has some questions for you."

"It'll only take a minute," Bolan told her. She was so nervous, her lower lip was quivering. Tears weren't far behind. "And don't worry, you aren't in any trouble."

"O-okay," she managed to say.

Bolan eyed Vahle and arched one eyebrow. "If we could have a few minutes…"

"Of course," Vahle said. He stopped in the doorway. "I'll be in my office if you need me." When he left, he closed the door firmly.

Bolan introduced himself, as he had at the school's office, as U.S. Marshal Matthew Cooper, an alias he had used many times. He'd wanted to talk to Tracy, whom the Fultons had identified as Angela's best friend, without her parents around. And he hadn't wanted to wait. He figured identifying himself as a marshal would get cooperation from the school administration, and he already had the necessary badge and

ID. He had sworn the school staff to secrecy, and hinted that it had something to do with Angela's death, but didn't reflect on Tracy at all.

Sometimes sticking close to the truth was easiest.

"Sit," he told Tracy now. "I just want to talk for a minute."

Tracy swallowed anxiously, but she sat.

"You knew Angela Fulton, right?" Bolan asked.

"She was my BFF."

"That's what I've heard."

"Is this about…what happened to her?" Tracy queried.

"Yes, it is. Were you there?" He already knew the answer.

"When she—"

"I know she was alone when she took her own life. I mean when she took the drugs. The Ivory Wave."

"I didn't…I mean—"

"I told you," Bolan said, "you're not in any trouble. I just need to know."

"We were at a party," Tracy said. "And somebody had some, and she…she wanted to try it."

"So she had never done it before?" Bolan asked.

Tracy's gaze rose to the ceiling, as if somebody had lowered a lifeline. "No."

Bolan stared at her. Her face flushed. "Okay, yeah, a few times. We both have."

"But this time was different?"

"Not for me. I think maybe she used more of it than she had before," Tracy replied.

"A lot more?"

"Not a whole lot, but some. She was kind of depressed over this guy. She said she wanted to forget about him. Forget about everything. So she wanted more, and she got more."

This was what Bolan had come for. "From whom?"

"Some guy at the party."

"What guy?"

"I don't remember," Tracy stated.

Again he didn't move his gaze from her face, didn't blink. He knew his stare could be intense when he wanted it to be. "Yes, you do."

"Okay, all right," she said. "It was Greg. Greg Reed. He always seems to have some."

"Just Ivory Wave, or other stuff?"

"Whatever somebody wants, Greg can usually get," Tracy told him.

His name wasn't on the list the Fultons had given Bolan. "Does he go to school here?"

"He used to. He dropped out a few years ago."

"He have a job?" Bolan queried.

"Mostly he hangs out, I guess."

"Where?"

"Wherever he wants. Parties. His place."

"Where does he live?" Bolan probed.

"You mean, like an address?"

"Exactly like that."

"He won't...I mean, will he know I told?"

"I'm not asking you to testify in court, Tracy. I just want to know where he lives. He'll never know how I found out."

"I don't know the address. It's this little house, like behind another house?"

"Tell me how to find it, then."

She gave Bolan directions and sketched out a map. He told her not to tell anyone about their talk, and thanked her for her time. Then he stopped by the front office and reminded Mr. Vahle to keep quiet about his visit.

He didn't know how his encounter with Greg Reed might go. But if it went the way he thought it might, it would be good if nobody mentioned his trip to the school. Or if they did, that the only name they knew was that of U.S. Marshal Matthew Cooper, who didn't exist.

Often, honesty really was the best policy, but there were times when a little misdirection was better.

REED LIVED IN a carriage house behind a larger house, in one of Makin's poorer districts. The main house was run-down, its yard brown and weedy, its paint peeling. The carriage house was even worse. Bolan was surprised the music blasting from inside wasn't literally shaking shingles off the roof.

He knocked, but no one answered. That didn't surprise him. After a minute, he tried the knob. It turned freely in his hand, so he went inside. The music was louder, all bass and driving drums. A singer with a deep voice was wailing about the silence of the grave. At this point, the idea of silence sounded pretty good. Bolan considered pulling the plug on the sound system, but then decided that he might be glad it was going, to drown out any other noises.

He found Greg Reed in a filthy bedroom, smoking a joint and looking at porn on a laptop. The kid was emaciated, all arms and legs and a willowy torso, with no meat on him anywhere. His hair was brown and straight, pasted to his scalp, and acne had had its way with his skin.

"You Greg Reed?" Bolan asked.

Reed jumped about six inches and slammed the computer shut. "Jeezus!" he cried. He spun around and looked at Bolan, dropping his joint to the floor and stepping on it at the same time. "Who the hell are you? What are you doing in here, anyhow?"

Bolan showed him the marshal's badge and ID. "United States Marshal Service," he said. "I knocked on your door, but you didn't answer."

"So you just barged in?"

"Bad habit." Bolan smiled. "Got a minute?"

"You got a warrant?"

"Let's not go down that road," Bolan said. "I'd rather have

a nice chat here than have to take you into custody, read you your rights, wait for a lawyer and all that."

"Start chatting," Reed said with a smirk. "I'll let you know if I decide I want a lawyer."

Bolan crossed muscular arms over his chest. "I'll let you know if I think you get one. You gave Angela Fulton some Ivory Wave at a party, right? Couple weeks ago."

"Maybe."

"Gave, or sold?" Bolan asked.

"I don't remember."

Bolan stepped closer, his full six-foot-three frame filling the small room.

"Greg, I already don't like you. Don't make it worse."

"Or what?"

"You don't want to know." The kid was maybe twenty, twenty-one at the most. Bolan didn't like him, but he didn't want to have to hurt him.

Reed took the hint. "Okay, I sold her some. I don't charge much for it, just enough to cover my costs and a little more. And it's not illegal."

"It's not," Bolan said. "But can you say the same about the other things you supply? You were smoking pot when I came in here."

Bolan used the tip of his boot to nudge a stack of papers that were thrown over a discarded bong.

"That's all I had. Personal use."

"Greg, don't try to be smart. It doesn't work on you."

"What's that mean?"

"It means I already know you deal. What I want to know is who supplies you."

"Ivory Wave is legal, dude. I get it at a store," Reed told him.

"Flat Water Smokes?"

"If you already have all the answers, what are you doing here?"

"What about the rest of it? What if you needed to supply some pot? Or some meth?"

"Who says I do?" Reed queried.

Bolan moved faster than the kid could anticipate. One instant he was halfway across the room, the next he had hauled Reed from his chair and was holding him by the T-shirt, his head almost brushing the ceiling, feet kicking well away from the floor. "Jeezus!" Reed said again.

"I'm starting to lose my patience with you. Are you going to answer my questions, or am I going to have to get angry?"

"Okay! Just put me down, dude!"

Bolan released him. The kid fell to the floor, stumbled, then regained his balance and sat on the edge of his bed. The soldier could see fear in his eyes now. "Well?"

"Look, I'm not like some big-time dealer or anything. I just try to help out my friends, right? When they need something."

"So anything legal, like Ivory Wave, you buy through legal channels?"

"That's right," Reed said.

"And other things? Not so legal?"

"I have a connection."

"Who?" Bolan asked.

"Do I have to say?"

Bolan moved fast again, snatching the laptop off the desk. A power cord snapped out of its slot. He let Reed see the laptop in his hand for a second, then he casually tossed it across the room. It hit a wall, then fell to the floor, landing on a corner. The corner caved in and the lid opened, showing a cracked monitor. Reed leaped up. "You broke my computer!"

"Better answer my questions while you still have a home. Who's your connection?"

"Jeez. It's my brother, okay? Paul. God, will he be pissed."

"Where does he get his supply?" Bolan asked.

"How would I know? He's eight years older than me. He knows people. If I need something, he can get it."

"Anything?"

"I don't know. I mean, I've never asked him for anything like crack or heroin."

"So you have standards, that's what you're saying?" Bolan queried.

"That's right."

"But you don't mind supplying poison to teenage girls?"

"I never sold Angela anything she hasn't used a dozen times."

"Who sold it to her the first time, then?"

Reed looked away. "Okay, maybe I did that."

"That's what I thought. For all practical purposes, Greg, you killed that girl."

Reed paused and stepped back, his eyes filled with tears. They started rolling down his face. "I d-d-didn't mean to. The shit lately has been different. I even told Angela to go easy because it's been so powerful."

"Then maybe you should have thought about what you were doing," Bolan suggested.

"I g-guess s-so, but this stuff, you know anyone can buy. I never really thought much about it. Not until Angie."

"Here's what I'm going to do, Greg," Bolan said. "I'm going to leave now. I want you to tell your brother that we talked. Tell him what you told me."

Reed sniffled. Snot smeared his upper lip. "He'll k-kill me!"

Bolan shrugged. "Maybe. Maybe not. But if you haven't told him by the time I talk to him, then I'll come back and do it myself."

He started for the door, then stopped, turned and pointed at the kid. "Don't think I won't," he said.

When he left, the music was still screeching.

6

He didn't really care about Greg Reed's brother Paul. If Paul wanted to kill Greg, Bolan wouldn't lose any sleep over it. But to run down every small-time dealer in the country would take the rest of his life, and by the time he finished, a new crop would have come along who were just as bad. He had to let some things go.

What he wanted was to find the source of the particular batch of Ivory Wave that had killed Angela Fulton. Legal or not, somebody had to pay for that, and he had a sneaking suspicion that the lab was going to come back with something a little more than the usual formula. Now he'd determined that it had come from the Flat Water head shop. And he already had an invoice and a bill of lading, so he knew the trucking company that delivered the stuff to the shop, and who had sold it. He went back to the motel and took out those documents.

The carrier was a company called Vandyke Freightlines. He had seen their trucks on the highways a million times, green eighteen-wheelers with a stylized Vandyke beard in their logo. According to the invoice, the Ivory Wave had come, along with assorted other items, from a distributor in Indiana called Devilweed, Inc. Bolan searched them online and learned that they distributed paraphernalia and assorted items to head shops, convenience stores, smoke shops and other businesses throughout the Midwest. All of it legal, as far as he could tell.

The legality of it wasn't what concerned him. He had already crossed into unlawful territory several times this day. The justice he had promised Eddie Fulton had nothing to do with laws that Congress had passed and judges upheld. It was a rawer, and maybe more pure, brand of justice.

He was just closing the laptop when the police knocked on the door to his room.

The soldier knew it was cops before they announced themselves, just by the sound of their footsteps outside—three men, in rubber-soled shoes or boots, all walking with determined purpose. Then one of them said, "Mr. Kenner, this is the Makin P.D. Open up, please," confirming his hunch. Kenner was the fake name he had given when he checked in, backing it up with a phony driver's license from Montana, and paying with a prepaid credit card that didn't have any name on it. Bolan didn't like leaving a paper trail, especially when he was working. And the Executioner was nearly always working.

Bolan glanced around the room quickly. His guns were zipped in a carry bag and hidden beneath the pedestal bed. Nothing incriminating was in view. He opened the door. "Something wrong, Officers?" he asked.

"You're Tom Kenner?"

"That's right."

"Got some identification?"

Bolan's wallet was on the little bedside table. He left the door open and fetched it. While he did, the cops came in. One of them closed the door. "Right here," Bolan said. He handed over the Kenner driver's license.

The cop who had done all the talking so far was older than the other two, in his early fifties. He had a creased, weathered face under short white hair. The others were both younger, and had the look of military men, straight backed, with eyes that didn't miss much. They were, Bolan thought, much like him.

The older one studied the license, then gave it back. "What brings you to Makin, Mr. Kenner?"

"Is there something wrong?" Bolan asked, ignoring the question. "Have I been accused of something?"

The older one turned to his companions. "He look right to you?"

The others nodded. "Mr. Kenner," the older one said, "I'm the police chief here. My name's Curtis Stiles, but you can call me Chief Stiles. I have a responsibility to this town and the people in it, and the businesses here. It doesn't matter that sometimes I don't much like the people or their businesses. And I believe that this morning you paid a visit to one of them, a place called Flat Water Smokes-n-Stuff. Kind of a hippie place, but they pay their rent and they pay their taxes. Is that correct?"

"I pay taxes, too," Bolan said. "And I think I know my rights. Are you arresting me for something?"

"We're just having a conversation here, Mr. Kenner."

"I don't have a lawyer here in Makin, but I'm sure I can get one," Bolan said.

"Let's don't be hasty," the chief said. "Here's the thing—Flat Water has a surveillance video system and a silent alarm. One of the boys tripped the alarm. By the time my officers got there, the owners had decided they weren't interested in pressing any charges. But the officers asked around at the other merchants, and somebody had spotted your car and made a note of the license plate. We didn't figure you for a local, so we checked the motels. Not that many to check, really."

"All right, maybe I did," Bolan said. "And maybe not. But if the shopkeepers aren't pressing charges—"

"We could still book you, and no doubt convict you," Chief

Stiles said. "But I'll tell you something. You might think I'm just a small-town police chief, and you'd be right. But that doesn't mean I ought to be underestimated. After all, I found you, didn't I?"

Bolan didn't answer, but he couldn't argue with the man's reasoning.

"So I thought about the business that you dropped in on, and I thought about what I saw on the videotape I made Zach show me while we waited for the paramedics to patch up his partner. You aren't just some guy who wandered into town, Mr. Kenner, or whoever you are. You're no traveling salesman. Then I called an old friend of mine. You might know him—his name's Eddie Fulton?"

Bolan tried to keep his expression blank. But the chief was studying him, and maybe there had been an inadvertent twitch of the eye, or flaring of a nostril. At any rate, Stiles took it as confirmation. "Yeah, I thought as much. So I thought about Eddie, and about Angela, who was one of the sweetest little girls I ever knew. I watched that girl grow up, you know that?"

"I do now," Bolan said.

"Yeah, well, I did. My own is just a year older. They were in Scouts together, school, all that. Anyway, I remembered what had happened to Angela, and I asked Eddie if he knew you. Of course, he wouldn't say one way or the other. Which, to me, said it all."

"So what now?" Bolan asked.

"Now I'm going to suggest that you get out of town. I've got no interest in hauling your ass down to the station, going to the trouble of arresting you and getting the courts involved. If you sort of lost patience over there at Flat Water and maybe made a little bit of a mess, I got no problem with that. Not, you know, considering how much I liked Angela and her folks."

Bolan caught the eye of one of the younger cops, who gave him a discreet nod. It was barely perceptible, just the slightest dip of his head. But it was enough to confirm that the chief was on the level, that his offer wasn't a trap or a game of any kind. One warrior to another. "Okay," Bolan said. "You've got a deal."

"That's what I wanted to hear," Chief Stiles said. "You'll be gone today?"

"Count on it."

"In that case, enjoy the rest of your brief stay." The chief gestured toward the door. One of the younger cops opened it and stepped out. The others followed. The chief stopped in the doorway, gave Bolan a last, appraising look, then closed the door.

7

Before the police showed up, Bolan had called Stony Man Farm and read off the DOT identification number on the bill of lading he had taken from the head shop. Now that Chief Stiles and his men had gone, he called Hal Brognola. "I've been asked to leave Makin," he reported.

"By whom?"

"The chief of police, for starters."

"What are you going to do?" Brognola asked.

"Leave Makin," Bolan said. "I think I'm done here, anyway."

"Didn't think they'd be able to chase you out, Striker."

"The rest of the story isn't here anyway. What did the lab come back with?"

"This is nasty stuff, but you're right about it not being the normal crap, which is bad enough," the big Fed said. "This stuff is laced with LSD."

"LSD?"

"Yeah, the lab guys ran it twice. The amounts aren't large enough to make anyone look real hard or for drug dogs to come back with, but it's there. The lab techs think it has to do with the addiction quality. The other stuff is addictive and acts a lot like meth, but this stuff adds an extra kick."

"Why hasn't it been picked up before?"

"In part because you're not dealing with an FDA-approved

pharmaceutical company. The crystals are unpredictable. One container might barely have any while another might be almost pure hallucinogen."

"Is the government willing to step in with this evidence?" Bolan asked.

"No. They need more. Their argument is that anyone along the way could have added the drugs. So if you can track down the source unofficially, I can make it official."

"That's fine. I'll get to the source. Any word on that truck I asked about?"

"Actually, yes," Brognola said. "It's got GPS, and Aaron's tapped into Vandyke Freightlines, via the Department of Transportation. The truck's headed your way."

Aaron "the Bear" Kurtzman probably knew more about the inner workings of most government agencies than the people who worked for them did, and he definitely knew more about their computer networks. "More precisely?"

Brognola read off some GPS coordinates, then chuckled. "In English, what that means is that it's on I-80, about thirty minutes outside Des Moines and headed west."

"So it is coming toward me."

"Doesn't mean it won't change course. But yes. Looks like it onloaded a shipment outside Cleveland and has been delivering orders throughout the Midwest, at cities along the I-80 corridor."

"So if I head east, I might be able to intercept it. As long as you guys keep me posted on its whereabouts."

"We're tracking it, so we can do that. No problem."

"All right," Bolan said. "I'm packing up and heading out. Talk to you from the road."

He was glad to be able to honor the chief's request. Chief Stiles might have considered it a command, but although Bolan didn't like pulling rank, the truth was that his pay grade was considerably higher than a small-town police chief's.

He was, as he'd told Brognola, finished with what he could accomplish in Makin anyway. The Ivory Wave didn't come from Makin, and its impact was being felt far beyond its city limits. No, he had to find out who was behind the plague, to do whatever he could to shut off the pipeline that pushed it out to where it could poison other kids, send other Angela Fultons to hospitals and morgues.

He carried his belongings to the rented car, checked out of the motel and made his way to the interstate.

As THE DAY wore on, Bolan passed through Lincoln and Omaha and into Iowa, with the sun at his back. Stony Man personnel kept him updated on the truck's progress. It had made some deliveries in Des Moines—or that was the assumption based on its travel pattern—then continued west on I-80. As darkness began to fall, Bolan got word that the truck had stopped again, at a truck stop on the edge of Stuart, Iowa. There was no way to know if it was there for the night or just for a dinner break, of course. But for the moment, at least, it wasn't budging.

Bolan had been driving at a steady speed, a few miles above the speed limit, trying to cover ground without attracting the attention of law enforcement. Now he pushed down harder on the accelerator, passing traveling families and big rigs wherever he could. He still kept an eye out for the law—not that a ticket made out to Tom Kenner or Matt Cooper would be a problem, but he didn't want to be delayed. Catching up to the truck while it was parked would be much easier than having to trail it until it stopped again.

As he neared Stuart, he learned the truck hadn't budged in forty minutes. Bolan silently urged the trucker to stay put a little while longer. Have a piece of pie, he thought. Another cup of coffee.

Soon he saw the glowing lights of the truck stop against

the dark eastern sky. He checked in once more, learning that the truck he wanted was still there. He pulled off the interstate and eased into the lot. The rental was low on gas, and he could use a meal and something to drink. But those things would have to wait. He was accustomed to that—his years as a soldier had taught him that the pleasures, even the necessities, of the body often had to be postponed until the mission was accomplished, or else dealt with hastily whenever the opportunity arose.

The truck stop had a gas station in front, with spaces for passenger cars and small trucks. Off to the left were stalls for bigger trucks. Behind that was a large, barnlike truckwash facility. A central building, well-lit, contained a convenience store and restaurant, and shower and other amenities for the truckers.

He drove slowly past row upon row of parked big rigs, watching for the distinctive green of a Vandyke vehicle. Truckers, most of them men, moved back and forth between their rigs and the buildings, carrying coffee or paper bags with meals in them. Bolan saw female truckers as well, dressed, like the men, in jeans and ball caps and coats or jackets against the chilly spring night. A couple of other women, wearing considerably less clothing—a miniskirt and stiletto heels, in one case, though she was an anomaly—were more likely lot lizards, prostitutes who worked the truck lots, servicing the men who drove the highways.

The first green truck he saw proved to be the wrong one, but after a few more tries, he spotted one that had the correct Department of Transportation number painted on it. He made a mental note of its position, then drove closer to the store and parked the rental. He put the Desert Eagle in a holster on his hip, his Beretta 93-R in a shoulder holster and his Cold Steel Tanto combat knife in its sheath above his ankle, then donned a dark blue windbreaker. His clothes were black, and he moved easily through the darkened lot, avoiding drivers when possible, and nodding casually to those he encountered. No one stopped him.

When he had made his way back to the truck he sought, he found it was empty. He checked the cab, tapped on the window in case the trucker was inside the sleeper. The trailer was locked up tight, with a padlock on the outside.

He didn't want to attract attention by breaking in, although he knew he could get the cab unlocked in a matter of minutes, if that. Instead, he stuck to the shadows and waited in the area, moving often, never drawing attention to himself.

Finally a guy walked toward the truck and pawed keys out of his pocket. Long brown hair beneath a Kenworth trucker's cap was still wet from a shower. The man held a huge plastic mug containing thirty-two ounces of some iced beverage, and he sipped from it, a plastic straw disappearing into a dense handlebar mustache. Not a Vandyke, Bolan noted, though he also had a soul patch under his lower lip. He was lean and tan, with a stringy muscularity that Bolan wouldn't underestimate. He unlocked the truck's cab on the driver's side.

Bolan moved fast, so that he reached the driver before he climbed up into the tractor. The guy had put his drink on the seat and was just about to heave himself up when Bolan got a hand on his shirt and yanked him backward, off the truck. He snaked a hand around the guy's mouth so he couldn't cry out.

"Is this your regular ride?" he asked.

The driver struggled against him, his eyes wide with fear. He was strong, as Bolan had guessed—it took a certain amount of strength to handle these big trucks, after all. The soldier asked again, and this time the guy nodded. "So you know what kind of poison you're hauling around?" Bolan asked.

The guy squirmed in Bolan's grasp. The soldier could easily snap his neck, or render him unconscious, but neither of those would provide him with the intel that he wanted. Instead, he was still holding the struggling driver when someone came around the end of another truck and saw them there.

"Hey!" the newcomer shouted. "There's someone bein' robbed over here!"

He charged toward Bolan and the Vandyke driver, screaming all the way.

"You don't know what's going on here," Bolan warned him. "Stay back!" He turned the Vandyke driver so that he could defend against this newcomer at the same time.

But then he heard running footsteps approaching, more people crying out. He could take them on, he knew. He had faced down groups of men before, and walked away. These were innocent men, though, and a couple of women. They weren't the enemy, just working people, coming to the aid of someone they thought was a peer in trouble.

Bolan had never been comfortable with the idea of collateral damage. His mantra was innocents wouldn't get hurt just because they were in his way. He tried to spin the driver he held, to use him as a shield to hold back the others. But there was no way to explain what he was doing, and by the time a dozen people had surrounded them, he knew he was going to have to escape, to try some other way of getting to the Vandyke driver. The important thing now was getting out without being arrested or hurting anyone.

He pushed the driver into the nearest onlookers and drew the Desert Eagle in the same swift motion. "Everybody stay back," he said. "You don't know what's going on here. You don't know what this guy is hauling, but it doesn't look like you're going to let me explain. I don't want to hurt anyone, so get out of my way and we'll just pretend this never happened."

The Vandyke driver took advantage of the moment to climb into his cab and start his engine.

"I don't think so, buddy," one of the other drivers said. "The cops are on the way."

"You can explain it to them," another one said.

Bolan could already hear sirens, and the Vandyke truck was pulling out. He holstered the weapon. He wasn't going to shoot anyone, not as long as there was another option. Someone grabbed him from behind and he caught the man's arm, performing a half spin and using him to flail at the people in front of him. He cleared a path, but instead of using it, he dropped to the ground and rolled beneath the nearest truck. The first one to try to follow got a boot in the jaw for his trouble. He fell back, bleeding from the mouth, and the others reacted to that just long enough to allow Bolan to get up on the other side and run between trucks for a minute. One driver tried to block his way, but a straight-arm to the upper chest put him down without even a chance to cry out.

When he was in the clear for a few seconds, the soldier went up a trailer and lay flat on its roof while people rushed by below. A police car showed up, red and blue lights tinting the sky beneath the glow of the truck stop's signs. One cop got out and started talking to the gathered drivers while the other stood next to their vehicle, aiming its side-mounted floodlight between the trucks.

From his vantage point atop the truck, Bolan could see the Vandyke rig making its way to the truck stop's exit. From there, it would have to travel a short spur road to the interstate, then climb up an entrance ramp, trying to gain speed all the way.

Bolan had three minutes. Maybe four, tops. The other truckers had mostly gathered around the cops, or gone back to their own rides. Bolan dropped back to the ground, as silent as a cat, and ran away from the truck stop toward the grassy stretch between tarmac and highway.

As he neared it, he saw the Vandyke truck turn onto the

ramp. Its headlights speared the sky as it started climbing. He could hear it ratcheting through the gears. He was running all out, hoping nobody was watching but unable to verify that without perhaps wasting a fraction of a second that he would need.

The truck was gaining speed. Bolan was at his capacity, and knew that the time he could keep it there was finite. He was breathing easily, his long legs scissoring through the dark night, away from the lights of the truck stop, but he could maintain that for only so long. He thought he had it timed right, but if the truck was able to gain more speed up the ramp than he guessed, this would be a long, hard sprint for nothing.

The driver shifted again, altering the pitch of the big engine's roar. The truck started to pick up speed. Bolan dug within himself for an extra measure of strength. He pumped his arms, felt his feet slamming into grass and then the hard roadway, felt the wind of the truck barreling past him, almost near enough to touch.

Then he slowed minutely and altered his path, because he was there, the truck hurtling past him. He came up behind it, knowing the timing had to be right, because he wouldn't get two chances.

Missing the first chance might just kill him.

He could sense the rig starting to pull away. He sucked in air, let it out and reached for the handle on the trailer's door. At the same instant that he closed his right hand around it, he got his left foot on the bumper and allowed his right one to leave the ground.

He was clinging to the back of the big rig, rapidly approaching interstate highway speed. Wind buffeted him, threatening to tear loose his grip at any instant. And between him and the driver in the tractor, there was still a forty-eight-foot trailer to get past.

Bolan had a feeling he was in for a long night.

8

Dominic Chiarello had continued earning while he was away—Nuncio and Artie kicked over to him, plus he had ongoing investments. But those earnings, while steady, had been static, if that. They didn't grow much, while in twenty-five years, prices on everything had gone up. Annamaria needed even more scratch just to keep the household running. If they'd ever had kids, it would have been worse yet.

So while his financial resources hadn't been entirely depleted, neither had they improved. And to launch a new operation—especially one that would, as he believed, lead to a full-scale war against his own brother—required cash.

Since he had people in his little group who were in tight with Nuncio, peeling some green away from his brother had a certain poetic justice that he liked.

The poker game was being held at a private home in Shaker Heights. It was a strictly middle-class ranch house in a strictly middle-class neighborhood. Nuncio had bought it years ago. Nobody lived in it full-time, but he let guys stay there if they were between homes, or if their girlfriends had kicked them out. And everybody used it when they needed someplace to go with a mistress, because it was cheaper and more discreet than a motel. As a result, it was definitely a guys' place, rarely cleaned, the walls plastered with pinups. There was a big living room facing the fenced backyard, where the pool and hot tub got a lot of use during the warmer months, and the game was held there.

On this night, eight guys were playing. Nuncio wasn't one of them, but the players were either members of his organization or their invited guests. They were all men, ranging in age from about twenty-five to fifty-five. All white. They were drinking bottled beer and laughing at dirty jokes. A thick haze of smoke hung in the air, and there were piles of cash all over the table.

Because they knew the layout, Artie and Nico went in through the front door, acting as if they had just come over to watch the action. At the same time, Chiarello, Dario and Massimo went around to the back. While Artie was regaling the players with a story about a stripper he had met, Nico feigned a coughing fit and unlocked the sliding glass door to the backyard, ostensibly to get some air.

And three men came inside, wearing rubber animal masks and holding automatic weapons. "Hands where I can see them," Chiarello growled. "Nobody be a hero—it ain't worth it."

Chiarello had expected everybody to be armed. In the old days, they would have been. But only one guy started to reach for a gun in a leather holster at the small of his back. Dario tapped him on the side of the head with the barrel of his Uzi machine pistol, and the guy let his hands go limp. A trickle of blood ran down the side of his face as Dario snatched the gun and pocketed it. The rest complained, but kept their hands flat on the table, even as Chiarello scooped their cash into a black plastic garbage bag. Nico and Artie stood back, hands raised, as if they were totally innocent.

"You got any idea whose place this is?" one of the older men asked. He looked vaguely familiar to Chiarello, but barely. Maybe he had known the guy when they were both young, but he couldn't place him now.

Chiarello, wearing a donkey mask that covered his entire head, just laughed. "Like I give a shit?" he said. "Shut up."

"You guys are dead," another one said. "Walking fuckin' dead men."

When the table was cleared off, Chiarello decided to take it a step further. "Now your wallets," he said. "On the table."

"No way!" one of the poker players protested. This time Massimo lashed out. He was carrying a MAC-10 with a suppressor and a 30-round magazine. He let go with one hand and smashed his fist into the guy's mouth. The guy spit blood, and a tooth came out.

So did his wallet. Nico and Artie both put theirs on the table, knowing, Chiarello figured, that they'd get them back. Once the other guys had all gone along with it, Dario picked up the wallets and tossed them into the trash bag.

They were about ready to leave when one of the younger men at the table looked at the jewelry on Massimo's hands. "Ain't that Ric's ring?" he asked. "That one with the eagle head. Who the fuck are you?"

Chiarello saw the change come over Massimo. He had been tense, but he suddenly loosened up. He was wearing a rubber rabbit mask, and the thing had a foolish grin. Chiarello thought maybe Massimo's face matched it at that moment.

"Smart guy," Massimo said. "Too bad for you."

At that, a couple of other players tried to dodge the inevitable. But Massimo's SMG was already in his hands and pointed at them. He squeezed the trigger and raked it across the table. Big .45ACP rounds plowed into skulls, filling the air with the pinkish mist of mixed blood, brains and bone fragments, One guy started to rise, and the rounds stitched down his sternum. Chiarello figured his autopsy would go quickly, since he had already been unzipped. At the last moment Nico and Dario joined in, but by then they were shooting at dead men.

"Don't waste your bullets!" Chiarello yelled. "Let's get out of here. We got what we came for." He was pissed off that it had gone down that way. He had wanted the men left alive, so they could bitch to Nuncio that someone had taken them down. Nuncio would still hear about it, but the slaughter might launch things on a trajectory that was faster and more dangerous than he had planned for.

Cigar and cigarette smoke still drifted in the air, but now it was mingled with the more acrid smell of gunfire and the stench of men who had lost control of bowels and bladders as they died. What had been a messy but jovial poker game had turned into a scene of carnage that could turn the stomach of even the most hardened man. Chiarello knew it was just a beginning, not an end. But it had come too soon and, standing there, smelling it and seeing it, he felt panic niggling at him.

He stepped out the back door, into the yard. The pool was covered, but the scent of chlorine still floated there, cutting the stink from inside. The others followed after a few moments, Massimo last. Chiarello shook the garbage bag. "This is what we came for," he said. "We got it. Let's go."

MASSIMO DIDN'T THINK he would ever come down from the buzz. It was a good thing Nico was driving, because if he'd had his foot on the accelerator, they would be going 120 miles an hour and climbing. Killing one guy with a knife had been a thrill, but killing eight at once was something else entirely. Another level. The vibration of the submachine gun had traveled up his arm and chest and into his heart, he thought, and it would never end. Watching the way the bullets had torn apart heads, blown through eyeballs and pulverized jaws had been the most incredible thing he'd ever witnessed. He loved sex, especially with Carla, but even that didn't leave him feeling like this had.

Uncle Dom was angry, that was clear. He had hardly said

a thing since they'd left. He would get over it, though. They'd made a pretty fair haul—a few thousand bucks, anyway. And Uncle Dom hadn't known everybody at the table, but Massimo had. Between him and Nico and Dario and Artie D'Amato throwing in with Uncle Dom, and then the guys Massimo's father had lost this night, they had put a significant dent in Nuncio's operation.

That part made him a little sad, that he had betrayed his own father in such a potent way. Fathers and sons always had complicated relationships, he figured, but he might have just thrown a few extra complications into this one.

Whatever. Nothing his father had ever shown him had made him feel the way he did now.

Eight dead men. He couldn't wipe the grin off his face.

9

Earlier in the evening, Bolan had climbed up the back of a truck.

Of course, there had been a dozen or so men chasing him then, and the truck had been parked.

This one, however, was racing down the interstate. Wind tore at him, trying to wrench him loose, and the rattling of the truck didn't help.

There was no way he would be able to climb this one. And if he didn't do something soon, he would be splattered all over the interstate.

For the moment, anyway, the highway was mostly empty. That, at least, would work in his favor.

If he couldn't go up and over—and at this speed, he couldn't get off and run up to the cab—he was left with only one option.

He would have to go through.

He drew the Desert Eagle. A bad ricochet here could kill him, he knew. Hell, the recoil from the big gun could be the final straw that blew him off the truck and onto the pavement. Still, it seemed like his best bet.

The padlock holding the trailer closed wasn't a good one. Presumably the driver, or the trucking company, figured that nobody would be stupid enough to try to break in. Certainly not at more than sixty miles per hour.

He aimed at the cheap lock, held tightly to a handgrip on the back of the trailer and fired. The gun boomed and tried to leap from his right hand. In the near darkness the muzzle flash seemed exceptionally bright.

The lock shattered like an ice cube hit with a hammer.

Now Bolan's biggest challenge was shifting his weight so he could roll up the door enough to get inside, without falling off. He picked the remains of the lock off the hasp and let them fall to the roadway. He gave the door a tug, and it didn't budge. He didn't have much leverage, since he was pressed up against the door to keep from flying free. But the soldier didn't give up.

He gave another yank, and this time the door slid up in its tracks, grudgingly, but a little. He pulled again.

The door slid open a couple of feet.

Good enough.

Bolan bent, knowing this moment would be trickiest and most dangerous of all. At the same instant, he released his handhold and pawed for something to grab inside the trailer, pushing off the bumper with his powerful legs. His upper torso went inside, but at the same moment the truck jolted and nearly threw him out. He caught the door with his left arm, slammed his right palm against the wooden floor and stayed in.

From there, he was able to get his legs inside.

Success.

BOLAN LAY THERE for a minute, letting his heartbeat and breathing settle. Even as they did, his mind was racing. He would have to call Stony Man and try to have someone retrieve his rental car from the truck stop before law enforcement opened it and found his clothing and weapons. And he had to figure out how to get from the trailer into the tractor, from the inside.

Or did he?

He found his footing. The rear door was still open a couple of feet, but it was quieter inside, free from the constant lashing of the wind. The engine noise and the rumble of wheels on the road were almost soothing.

The trailer was loaded with pallets, wrapped in transparent plastic shrink-wrap. Each row of merchandise was packed tight and cleared just below the trailer ceiling.

Bolan slid the combat knife from its sheath and cut through the shrink-wrap on one of the pallets, several back from the door. He didn't want to risk anything sliding out of the back, and he needed the door slightly open in order to let ambient light from outside illuminate his task. His flashlight, like most of his other equipment, was in the rental car he had abandoned.

Beneath the wrap were stacks of cardboard boxes. Most of the boxes had logos that Bolan didn't recognize, so he slashed a few open. As he had suspected, the truck was making deliveries to head shops. The cartons contained growing equipment for pot farmers, cases of incense, pipes and bongs in layers of packing materials and more. Finally he opened a box that contained more boxes, these with the distinctive appearance of Ivory Wave packaging.

That gave him a new idea. He crouched near the open door, and saw that the highway behind them was still empty. Then he returned to the opened pallet and selected a box containing fragile grow lights. He gave it a gentle toss. It hit the trailer floor and then slid through the opening, falling to the road with a crash that Bolan could barely hear over the road noise. He looked out the back and saw the box bouncing along, tearing open, and the lights inside scattering across the highway.

It was a good start, but he had a way to go. Next he threw two boxes out the back. The truck continued barreling along at the same speed, so presumably the driver hadn't yet noticed.

Looking out the rear, Bolan saw headlights, still well off but moving up fast. Law enforcement? Bolan put together a quick plan. He could hide behind the pallets to dodge the trooper's first cursory glance. After that, the officer would go to the cab, where likely the driver would be stepping down, unless he had already been ordered to stay put with his hands sticking out the window. During the moments they were on the driver's side of the truck, Bolan could slip out of the back and go to the other side. Depending on how noisy the more involved search of the back might be, there was a possibility that he'd be able to slip in through the passenger door, and wait in the sleeper until the trooper was gone and the driver was on the road again.

Worst case, he'd be stranded alongside Interstate 80 with no wheels, watching the taillights of the truck as it drew away. He would try to ensure that that wasn't the case.

But the car hurtling toward them wasn't law enforcement at all. It was a BMW, a convertible, though with the top up against the still-cool springtime night. Looked like two passengers, though there could have been more. Bolan could make out only silhouettes at this point.

They came on fast, though, blinking headlights and honking like mad. As they pulled close, Bolan could see that the passenger was a buxom blonde. She was wearing a low-cut tank top, but approaching the truck, she yanked it down, exposing heavy, round breasts. She pressed them up against the passenger window, completely unaware that there was anyone in the trailer to see—though not likely to object, had she known. Then they were out of sight, but Bolan could tell by the sound that they were running alongside the cab for a minute or so before pulling away with a final honk. He had thought the honking and flashing had to do with the detritus landing all over the highway, but apparently it was just a sexual game she and the driver played, turning truck drivers into nothing but objects with eyes. Some of them would welcome the diversion, and the view. The road could be a lonely place, and a quick view of female flesh might be better than nothing on a cold night.

Bolan figured the odds were better than even that the driver was more focused on his window, and possibly his mirror, than he had been a few minutes earlier. Just in case, he hurled out three boxes, one right after the next, trying to get them to land to the truck's left side. They hit and flew apart, shedding their contents all over the highway.

The BMW raced ahead, doubtless looking for the next trucker to flash. Bolan threw another box out. Whether the driver stopped or not, he was taking a certain perverse pleasure out of destroying the head-shop merchandise.

This time, it seemed to have an effect. The trucker hit his air brakes hard enough to nearly knock Bolan off his feet. He flexed his knees and rode the jolt, then, as the truck slowed and pulled over to the shoulder, hazard lights flashing a warning to the empty stretch of highway, he drew the Desert Eagle and moved to the door. When he heard the driver's door, Bolan dropped to the ground, as silent as a falling feather. He stepped to the far side of the truck and waited.

The driver made it around the corner, boots crunching gravel. He said, "Shit..." and put his hands on the platform, preparatory to climbing into the back.

Bolan stepped into view. "Looks like you dropped something," he said.

Startled, he turned and saw Bolan. "You...?"

"You ready to continue our conversation?"

"Who the hell are you?"

Bolan showed him the big handgun. "That's not important. What's important is that you answer my questions without wasting any more time."

"I don't have to—"

Bolan wagged the barrel of the gun. "Yes, you do."

The guy dropped his hands to his sides. "What?"

"How much do you know about what you're hauling?" Bolan asked.

"It's shit for these hippie places. I pick it up at a distribution warehouse and I drive it to the stores. Park in the alley or loading dock if they got one, get it off the truck. Once it's on the ground, it's theirs."

"You know what's in the boxes?"

"I know how many boxes," the driver replied. "They're packed at the warehouse, put up on pallets and wrapped up. Could be piñatas, all I know."

"Piñatas? You think that's likely?"

"No, sir, I don't. Just saying is all."

Bolan had noticed before how staring into the deep, dark barrel of a Desert Eagle could make people unusually polite. He knew from hard experience that when one was pointed at you, the diameter of that opening looked about the same size as an oil pipeline.

"So what you're telling me is you never see inside the boxes. You don't take a look at the bills of lading you have people sign? You don't ever stop in the store for a while, sample the wares? When you're up there in that cab, shifting through the gears and resting your hands on the wheel, what goes through your mind? Memorizing Bible verses, that kind of thing?"

"Look, mister, if I knew what the hell you wanted from me, maybe I could help you out. But I don't. I mean, yes, sometimes if somebody offers me a little weed, I'll toke up. But not behind the wheel. And I never touch the merch in the truck. I'm responsible for that."

Bolan jerked a thumb toward the road. A pickup truck was racing past. "You dropped some," he said.

The driver looked at the dark highway. "You're gonna get me fired, man."

"I don't have to," Bolan said. "You just quit."

"What?"

"Give me your driver's license. Take whatever personal items you absolutely need out of the truck, but leave the paperwork."

"No way, man. That's—"

"I'm not asking," Bolan said. He wagged the Desert Eagle again. "Let's go. Time's wasting."

A FEW MINUTES later, Bolan was behind the wheel of the truck, driving east on the highway. He worked his phone out of his pocket and called Stony Man. After a minute, he had Kurtzman on the line. "You know that truck you've been tracking for me?" Bolan asked.

"Yeah, what about it?"

"Don't bother."

HAVING DISABLED THE truck's GPS device, Bolan drove through the night, trying to put miles between him and the trucker— whose name, according to the driver's license now in Bolan's pocket, was John Daggett—he had left on the side of the highway.

Daggett had gathered his personal belongings and stuffed most of them into a duffel bag, bundling the rest up in a blanket. Bolan had suggested that he call Vandyke Freightlines and let them know he was quitting after he delivered his current load, but without going into details about why. He warned that if Daggett reported his rig stolen while Bolan was driving it, he would find the trucker and kill him. He flicked the driver's license a couple of times. "After all," he said, "now I know where you live."

"Look, man, I didn't ask for none of this," Daggett said. "You've got no cause to be threatening me. I need this job."

"As long as you do the right thing," Bolan said, "we don't have a problem. I just want to make sure you believe me when I tell you that we will definitely have a problem if you cross me."

Daggett held his eyes for a remarkably long time. Bolan knew he could be intimidating; he cultivated it, in fact. Most people backed down much more quickly. "You don't have to worry about me, Jack. I don't even want to think about you again."

"You'll find work," Bolan said by way of parting. He got in the truck and keyed the ignition. He believed it, too. Daggett had some spine to him. He was glad he wasn't involved in Angela's death and he was pleased that Daggett was no more than a drop-and-go guy. He paused and turned to look at him before he pulled out. "A man named Hal is going to be giving you a call. He'll set you up with another job. This won't affect you at all."

"Yeah, sure he will."

"Daggett, you've only just met me, but do you have any doubt of my resolve?"

The trucker paused and stared long and hard at Bolan. "No."

"Expect the call."

AROUND THREE IN the morning, Bolan pulled off the highway at a lonely rural exit. Farm roads ran straight through the fields forever, as far as he could tell in the light cast by the sinking moon. There might have been nobody alive for a hundred miles in every direction.

He followed one of those roads until he found a smaller one, dirt, leading to a fallow field that had been plowed under and waited to come back into some farmer's rotation. Maybe it wouldn't produce for the farmer this year, but Bolan could get some use out of it. The ground was hard-packed enough for him to drive on, so he did, getting the rig out toward the middle of the field, far from anything flammable.

That part was key.

He stopped the truck, went to the back and removed the jerry-rigged strap he had tied on to hold the door closed. He shoved the door up its tracks, opening the trailer wide. Then he climbed back up and threw all the boxes of merchandise out into the field. They landed in a haphazard pile, and the more he tossed out, the higher the pile became. That was the idea, because fire liked to climb.

Bolan had a couple of gasoline containers on board that he'd stopped to fill up. He'd found a length of rubber hose, and he used it to siphon off more gas from one of the farmer's work trucks that had broken down at some point and been left for dead. He soaked the boxes, paying special attention to the ones containing Ivory Wave. When he'd used up his supply of fuel, he moved the truck a hundred feet away from the pile and walked back. He found a well-soaked small box, one that would burn fast but could be easily thrown, and carried it a dozen feet away. He lit it and hurled it onto the pile.

Then he hit the dirt, facedown.

The gasoline ignited like an incendiary device, with a whoosh and a wall of heat and flame that hit with force. Bolan felt it pass over him. Within moments it was more concentrated, rising from the boxes, a fiery updraft that carried sparks and embers into the sky. He had hoped he was far enough removed from civilization that no one would see the fire, but looking at it now, he realized that it was a bigger, brighter flame than he'd expected.

No matter. The Ivory Wave would burn first, and if someone wanted to battle the flames enough to get a brass pipe or

a bong, it was his or her funeral. He got back into the truck,
started it and headed for the highway.

AN HOUR LATER Bolan pulled into a roadside rest area. Other
trucks already filled some of the long, slanted spaces, so his
wouldn't stand out. He needed sleep and sustenance, even if it
was just snacks from the vending machines. Sometimes food
trucks—"roach coaches"—worked rest areas in the mornings,
so he might be able to grab something more closely resem-
bling a meal then. Whether he did or not, he planned to be
back on the road around sunrise. Someone from Stony Man
Farm would alert him if Daggett went back on his word and
reported the truck stolen, or if the people at Vandyke realized it was on the move. Unless that happened, he needed to
keep covering the miles.

   He climbed into the truck's sleeper. Long years of combat
experience had taught him how to fall asleep fast, whether
he slept for fifteen minutes, an hour, or more. Most people
in the civilian world had at least some idea of how long they
would be able to sleep at a stretch, and when the next opportunity might come along. The same wasn't true for Bolan. He
had a couple of hours until the sun came up, and he would
use them to recharge his batteries. After that, he had no idea
when he would be able to close his eyes again.

10

Nuncio Chiarello stood in the living room of his Shaker Heights pad, his fists clenched in rage that had nowhere to go. Morning light streamed in through the sliding glass doors, illuminating a scene out of a nightmare.

There were eight dead men in the room, most of them friends and business associates. In earlier days, he would have referred to them as "soldiers," but he had tried hard to put that era behind him. He was a businessman now, not a Mob boss. These men were employees and colleagues, not gun-toting thugs. Yet although he and they had forsworn violence, it had found them anyway.

The walls around the poker table were pocked with bullet holes, plaster torn apart and crumbling, blood painting every surface. Some of the fine sprays had run, creating fringed arcs of red like something out of an abstract painting. In other spots, the blood had hit in thick swatches, as if someone had been trying out paint samples.

The bodies were similarly haphazard. They were sitting in chairs or sprawled on the floor. One man was missing so much of his face that Nuncio couldn't recognize him; slugs had torn his jaw off his face and obliterated both eyes. Flesh hung in ragged flaps over shattered bone and glistening muscle. He had dark blond, curly hair, leading Nuncio to think that it was a guy named Spratt who owned a regional chain of discount appliance stores that Nuncio had an investment in. His stocky build backed up that belief.

Brendan, who had skipped the game but called one of his buddies to check in around midnight, and then come over to see why he wasn't answering his cell, said that none of the corpses had wallets on them. And there were no winnings on the table, just a few bills scattered here and there. It was always possible that Brendan had pocketed all the cash before he made the phone call that had awakened Nuncio and left him with several hours of restless sleep. Come morning, as soon as he'd had a shower and a cup of rich Italian roast, he had come over. Now that coffee was mixing with his stomach bile, turning into acid that threatened to eat right through organs and bone and flesh and slosh out onto the floor.

Nuncio's sons, Gino and Massimo, stood off in the kitchen with Brendan, talking in low tones and letting Nuncio see the carnage for himself. These were men Nuncio trusted, but then, so were the dead. Again, in days gone by, the dead men would have had heaters of their own, probably sitting on the table next to their stakes, and the heist might not have ended the same way.

"How the hell did they get in?" Nuncio called. "The fuckers who did this?"

Brendan emerged from the kitchen. "When I got here, the back door was wide open," he said. He crossed the room, careful to avoid walking in blood, and pointed to a trail leading to the glass doors. "Look here, a cat or something came in after it happened. His footprints led out onto the grass in back before I lost them."

"I don't care about a damn cat," Nuncio said. "I want to know who did this."

Brendan shrugged, a casual gesture that infuriated Nuncio. "Could have been just about anybody, I guess," he said.

"Anybody who heard about the game would know there was gonna be some cash in play."

"This wasn't a major-league game," Nuncio countered. "It wasn't penny ante, but these guys played for twenties and fifties, not serious coin. Whoever did this probably got away with a couple grand, if that. Nothing worth eight lives."

Brendan's shoulders started to move again, but he caught himself in time. "Junkies, maybe," he said. "Couple grand to them would seem like a big payday."

"How would junkies hear about the game? Besides, everyone in town knows that you stay away from the product. The most they would find is a dime bag of weed or maybe a line of coke."

"I don't know, Nunce. I don't know what to tell you. Somebody found out about it and they hit it. You're gonna need CSI or some shit to figure out who."

"Go to the cops? Are you kidding me? I don't want anyone looking at the business."

"Hey, you're a legitimate businessman. You own this house. Some guys who were staying here decided to play some low-stakes poker—that's not your fault. But this is a multiple homicide. I don't even know how you would keep it quiet. Some guy's wives are gonna start wondering why they haven't come home. Might as well report it and get out in front of the problem. Otherwise it's likely to bite you on the ass."

Nuncio went to the glass door and opened it again, putting his own fingerprints on the handle, he knew, but he had already done that without thinking, when he'd first arrived. As if the killers might still be out back, taking a dip in the pool, maybe, or relaxing in the hot tub. He stepped outside, inhaled the brisk morning air and pondered Brendan's suggestion.

Calling the police wasn't a decision that came easily to him. The way Brendan laid it out, though, seemed to make sense. Even a guy with some history, which he couldn't deny he had, could be a victim of a crime. In this case, it was more to do with his house, anyway—a house in which he didn't even live. His guests, who were also employees, legally on the company's books, taxes withheld, the whole deal, had been killed. Brendan was right. The law would have to know.

Still, inviting cops into his life could only bring trouble. He turned back to the door. "You guys!" he called.

The three men came through the open door.

"Go over this house, top to bottom," Nuncio instructed. "If there's anything that even hints at illegal activity, any dope or anything, get it out. I want this place as anonymous as a motel room. And nothing, I repeat, nothing that leads back to our production."

The men nodded their understanding and went to work. Nuncio's businesses were, as Brendan had said, legit. But many of them had roots in less legitimate soil, and many of his employees were, not that long ago, simple thugs. These three, Brendan, Massimo and Gino, still carried everywhere they went—and Nuncio didn't like to step out his door without at least one of them by his side. He didn't carry a piece himself, because that being revealed would undermine his claim on legitimacy. But his own house was still a virtual armory, and not all of those weapons had been legally acquired.

He had become, by and large, a legitimate businessman. He didn't really consider adding a little something special to make his product stand out too ambitious, just profitable. That didn't put him above taking shortcuts, though. The habits of a lifetime—literally, of *lifetimes,* since his had been a multi-generational crime Family—were hard to break.

He went back into the house and found Brendan in one of the bedrooms, carefully checking dresser drawers for anything that might be incriminating. "Just toss the place," Nuncio said. "It'll look like the robbers did it."

"There are eight bodies in the house," Brendan said. "If

the cops think the killers went past the living room, they'll look for evidence in these other rooms. I don't want them to find my prints and nobody else's. Better we tell them the other rooms weren't touched."

Nuncio considered his argument. "Yeah," he said. "You're right. How much longer you figure this'll take? I got other stuff to do."

"Not today," Brendan said. He pulled a drawer out of the dresser and checked the bottom.

"What do you mean?"

"When the cops get here, you gotta be here. Your prints are all over the place, on top of any prints the killers might have left. You try to convince the law that you came in and saw that mess, then went to work, they're not gonna buy it. If you're not here, you become suspect number one."

"But if I am here, I'm not?"

"If you're here with witnesses, and no piece, and no powder residue on your hands or clothes, it'll look a lot better."

Brendan was a smart kid, and Nuncio knew he was right. Time was, he would have thought of all that himself. But now his head was full of invoices that had to be paid and bills that had to be collected, of payroll and inventories and taxes and license renewals. One thing he had never realized about the straight life was how much more complicated it was than the alternative.

If they got a line on who had done these murders, he would have to revisit old ways, at least for a while. Nobody could be allowed to get away with an all-out attack on his interests that way. And letting the courts deal with them wasn't good enough.

Blood had to be answered with blood. Some traditions didn't die.

"I'm glad I got you guys at my back," Nuncio said to Brendan. "You and my boys. Makes me feel a whole lot safer, I'll tell you that."

"Safer?" Brendan echoed. "You think there's gonna be more?"

"I don't know," Nuncio replied. "But in the old days, a hit like this only meant one thing. Someone was starting a war."

11

Devilweed Inc.'s warehouse was on Adams Center Road, where the sprawl of Fort Wayne, Indiana, began to thin as it stretched out toward New Haven. There was a barnlike auto-parts store next door. The warehouse was a plain concrete block building, two stories tall, with a steel roof. Bolan had parked the Vandyke truck a few blocks away and walked over to check it out.

The bills of lading he had found at Flat Water Smokes-n-Stuff and in the truck all pointed him toward Devilweed. It wouldn't be the original source of the Ivory Wave, he was convinced. The distribution company no doubt ordered from dozens of businesses, and took orders from dozens more. The proprietors of Devilweed were probably middlemen taking their cut from the toxins they peddled while hiding behind the wall of legality, but how deep the connection went was about to be revealed.

"Legal" and "right" went out the window when Hal Brognola came through with the content information. If the warehouse honchos were oblivious to what was in the crates they were shipping, Bolan would simply get rid of the offending substance; if not…Bolan intended to teach the folks at Devilweed the error of their ways. He wouldn't be able to cut off all avenues for the drug until he hit the manufacturer, but he had no problem putting up a giant roadblock to slow it.

From the outside, the warehouse looked like a single-story structure, because there were no windows on either level to provide scale, just a double steel-and-glass door facing the street. But he figured that while it would have high ceilings, it might also have a loft area, maybe even ringing the whole interior. Keep the offices off the warehouse floor, give the bosses a bird's-eye view of the help. The left side of the building—the north side—was one big loading dock with multiple bays. The right was as blank as the front. Bolan couldn't see the back without walking around, and the security cameras mounted at the roof line and pointed at the parking lot gave him pause. And he couldn't see inside from here, which was a disadvantage. Bolan always liked to study the lay of the land if he could, before that knowledge—or its lack—turned into a life-or-death matter.

As he stood there watching workers load two Vandyke trucks at the loading docks, the soldier had an idea. He had fought and slept in his clothes, and hadn't showered for some time, so he figured he looked the part. He shrugged, as if he had just reached a decision—not that it appeared anyone was watching him, but why take chances—and walked straight to the nearest loading dock. There he hoisted himself up onto the dock platform and started toward the first truck. Bay doors were open between here and there, so he glanced inside as he passed each door.

The layout was pretty much as he had expected. The main floor was full of steel shelving units, on which cardboard boxes of merchandise were stored. He saw a ball-bearing conveyor along the far side and curving toward him, leading toward a packing area. That butted up to the shipping area, which was close to the doors. On the far side was a loft-type arrangement with a steel gridwork and what looked like a concrete walkway running past offices.

One of the employees, a scrawny, long-haired guy in a

Devilweed T-shirt and ragged jeans, came out an open door. "Help you?" he asked.

"I was just wondering if they were hiring in there," Bolan said.

"Not that I know of."

"Anybody I could ask? Who would know for sure? A manager or something?"

"The owner's Jed Fowler," the guy said. "But he's out right now."

"I could check back later. There a good time to catch him?"

"Can't really say. Sometimes he's here, sometimes he ain't. But I would have heard if we had any openings."

"Okay," Bolan said. "Thanks anyway." He dropped off the side of the platform and walked back to the street, then away in the same direction he had been heading originally. Even if a security person was watching the monitors, nothing he had done would look particularly suspicious. He had hoped the guy would invite him inside the warehouse while he looked for a manager, but the glimpses he did get were better than nothing.

Besides, he couldn't stay too long, because he had an appointment.

THE MOTEL, IT turned out, wasn't far away, on East Tillman. There was a large parking area behind it, hidden from the street by a building that wrapped around an inner courtyard with a pool. Bolan parked the truck there and dialed a phone number. "Room 103," he was told. He hung up, got out of the truck and crossed the parking lot. The room faced toward the back of the building. When he reached it, the door opened and Charlie Mott stood inside.

"Striker," he said. "Good to see you."

"You don't want to smell me," Bolan said. "The water hot in this place?"

"So far." Mott still had his military bearing, though he had allowed his hair to grow out a little. His face was clean-shaven, and Bolan could see the tracings of fine scars around his nose and mouth. Mott had seen combat, and plenty of it.

Inside, Mott pointed to three bags on the floor, two of Bolan's and one other. The Stony Man pilot had flown into the Greenfield Municipal Airport in Iowa, rented a car and raced to Stuart. There he had emptied out Bolan's rental, then called the rental company and told them where they could pick it up. After driving back to the airport, he had flown into Fort Wayne, bringing with him a few other items Bolan had requested, from Stony Man's armory. While Brognola couldn't officially sanction the mission, he wouldn't leave Bolan out in the cold, with a cop's daughter dead and justice to be served.

"There's your stuff."

"Any problems?"

"Nada."

"Thanks," Bolan said. "I know it was a pain."

Mott's hard face broke into a grin."You kidding? There's not much I like to do more than flying, and the few things on that list, nobody will pay me for."

"Well, I appreciate it just the same. Would have been bad if that stuff had fallen into the wrong hands."

"You need anything else?"

Bolan knew what he meant. Mott was a good guy to have on your side in a fight. He had plenty of combat experience, and he never backed down. But although he was good at it, that wasn't what he loved. He loved being airborne, with the wind under his wings and the world spread out below him. Bolan thought it was a way of getting some distance from the things he had seen and done. Finding a new perspective. He didn't respect the man any less for it. "No," he said. "I think I'm good."

"If you're sure."

"Yes," Bolan said. "You spending the night?"

"I'm all fueled up and ready to go," Mott replied.

"Time for dinner?"

"Not if I'm getting home before midnight," Mott said. "Besides, nobody should have to eat with you until you've had that shower."

Bolan couldn't argue. He shook the big pilot's hand and watched him go.

HE WENT BACK to the Devilweed warehouse after a shower, a meal and several cups of coffee. He felt sharper and cleaner and ready for action. He had on his blacksuit and fine black leather gloves, and though he wished he had a smaller, less distinctive vehicle, he had a zippered leather bag in the truck's cab containing everything he thought he might need. He had already detached the trailer so he could use the tractor alone when he drove around town.

Between the shower and dinner, he had called the distribution company and asked to speak to Mr. Fowler. The manager had come back from wherever he had gone, and Bolan had identified himself as Tom Kenner, a man who was planning to open a new smoke shop in the Chicago suburbs. He said he was in town only for the evening, and if Mr. Fowler could spare him a few minutes, he'd like to discuss opening an account with the company.

When he arrived—again, parking the truck out of sight of the building—he brought his zippered bag and moved through the shadows. He didn't really want to open an account, so it wouldn't matter that when Fowler saw him he wouldn't be dressed or equipped like any other head-shop owner in history.

He reached the front door and tried it, finding it locked. Lights burned inside, though, and a car was parked outside the front door, so chances were Fowler was inside waiting for him, and wouldn't have set the alarm. The lock was nothing sophisticated, and a minute's effort with a rake and a tension tool took care of it. Bolan pushed the door open just enough to slip inside.

The main bank of overhead fluorescent fixtures was turned off, but there were lights on upstairs in a couple of the offices. Bolan had seen only one car, and he hoped Fowler was here alone. If he wasn't, then it would be a bad night for more than just the owner. Bolan walked between the shelving fixtures, spotting a section packed with boxes of Ivory Wave, waiting to be shipped out across the country.

Satisfied, he climbed the stairs.

At the top, the row of offices stretched away from the staircase. The door to the second office was open and light spilled from inside. Bolan heard voices as well, soft whispers. He moved silently to the door and looked in.

A man was sitting at his desk, with a woman sitting on his lap, or near enough. He looked as if he might have been a hippie once—a recovering hippie, Bolan thought. His hair was mostly gray but with a few dark patches, and it was on the longish side, covering his ears and curling where it reached the collar of his company-logo polo shirt. He had a tattoo on his right forearm, mostly covered by dark tangled hair. Bolan could see that arm, because he had it wrapped around the woman and it faced the door. The other hand was lost inside her blouse. There was plenty of territory there to get lost in.

She had dark brown hair and wore the pale pink shirt the man was mining beneath, and what looked like designer jeans. She was slender but curvy, and if Bolan was any judge of body language, everything that was going on between them was the man's doing, and not hers. She was going along with it, but not by choice. Bolan's guess was that the man was Fowler, the big boss, and she let him have his way with her in order to protect her paycheck.

That was how it looked to Bolan, anyway. The guy moved his head in to nip at her neck and she flinched, then gave a phony-sounding giggle, as if to say she was only playing hard to get but didn't really mean it when she tried to avoid his lips.

Bolan stepped into the room, tired of the game. "Are you Fowler?"

Startled, the man came up out of his chair, tipping the woman off his lap. She stumbled and hit the side of her head against his desk. "Who the hell are you?" the man asked.

"Are you Fowler?" Bolan asked again.

"Yes, okay, I'm Fowler. Are you Kenner?"

Bolan ignored the question and knelt beside the woman, who was sitting up and rubbing her head. "Are you okay?"

"Yes, thanks," she said. She had a sweet smile, with one front upper tooth that snagged her lip. "I'm such a klutz."

"My fault," Bolan said.

Fowler was standing up, staring at Bolan, who didn't look at all like a customer. A scowl worked its way across his face. "What do you really want, Mr. Kenner?"

Bolan helped the woman to her feet. "I think it might be a good idea if you left," he said to her.

She looked at Fowler, as if for permission. "Don't bother with him," Bolan said. She took his meaning and hurried from the office. In another moment, he heard her footsteps clicking down the stairs. He was quiet for another minute, until he heard the shush of the front door. Then he turned back to Fowler.

"What the hell do you mean by showing up here like this?" Fowler demanded. "Peggy works for me. You don't tell her what to do."

"I don't think that'll be an issue much longer," Bolan said.

"What does that mean?"

"I'll be asking the questions from now on," Bolan told him. "And I suggest you answer promptly and honestly."

Fowler reached for the cell phone on his desk. "I think I'll call the police now—"

Bolan moved faster than Fowler could even see, snatching the phone from his hand and hurling it against the far wall of the office. "Hey!"

The soldier shoved him back down in his chair. "How much Ivory Wave do you move?"

"What do you mean?"

Bolan smacked him across the mouth once. "Answer my question."

"I don't know, a lot," the guy said. "A couple thousand cases a year, anyway. I don't know the total weight because I don't know what's in a package. Twenty-four packages per case, so whatever that is. I got a deal with my cousin to be the exclusive distributor for the Northwest. We'll probably double before the end of next year."

"And that doesn't bother you?"

"Should it? It's a nice piece of change."

"It's killing people, Fowler."

"Look, everything we sell is perfectly legal."

Bolan shook his head. "I keep hearing that, but what you have here isn't exactly as legal as you guys have made it out to be, is it? I know about the drugs."

"Hey buddy, you got it all wrong. You can even bring dogs in here to search the place. Ain't nothing that they'd find."

"Only because you've hidden it so well. It's killing people, Fowler. Did you hear me?"

"About killing people?"

"Right."

"Anything can kill if it's misused," Fowler said. "You can kill someone with a box of chocolates."

"You're missing the point. You're selling poison, and people are using it as intended, and they're dying from it. The legality of it isn't the issue. Just because the authorities haven't caught on to your scam yet doesn't make it a nonissue. Dead people in graves are the issue here."

"None of that's my fault. If we weren't selling it, someone else would."

"That's the oldest excuse in the world," Bolan replied.

"You have a problem with free enterprise?"

"Not at all."

"What, then?"

"I have a problem with kids dying too young," Bolan said. "Seems like something that every decent human being ought to understand."

Fowler's expression was between fear and loathing, but he seemed to be trying to make himself look meaner than he felt. He crossed and recrossed his arms and swallowed hard.

"I guess we'll just have to agree to disagree. Is there something else you need, or do you want to get out of my place of business now?"

"Oh, we're a long way from done." He hadn't been able to determine, either from the packaging or the paperwork he had picked up in Makin, where the stuff was manufactured, and by whom. There was no brand name on the package other than IW Labs, which he guessed stood for Ivory Wave. He had asked the experts at Stony Man Farm to look into it, and even they had come up blank. IW Labs wasn't a corporation or a registered "doing business as" anywhere. "Where do you get your supply?"

"We buy it. I told you, I got a cousin," Fowler said. Instantly he braced for impact, as if he knew that he had just earned another blow. Bolan stood back with his hands on his hips and a wry smile on his face.

"Might be easier if I let you hit yourself," Bolan said. "But that would deprive me of a certain amount of pleasure. You know what I mean. And if you buy it, that means you've got records, contact information. I need to know where it comes from."

"Why should I tell you?"

"Because if you don't, then there'll be nothing at all keeping you alive. Does that sound like a good reason?"

"Bullshit! You'd actually kill me over that? I don't think so," Fowler said.

"In a heartbeat."

"Look, my sources are confidential. There are certain people that like to remain anonymous. I do my job and I get paid."

Bolan slid open his jacket to reveal his Beretta 93-R and cocked an eyebrow.

Fowler gestured toward a filing cabinet. "I've got their information in there."

"Get it."

Bolan moved close enough to grab the man if he needed to. He was sure Fowler had the information on his computer, too. If he wanted to pull a paper copy, that would be easier for Bolan to take with him. But if he went for anything else in the cabinet, like a gun, he wanted to be able to reach Fowler before he could use it.

"That woman," Bolan said while Fowler riffled through the files.

"Peggy?"

"Yeah. It appears that she doesn't like you."

"I know that."

"But you force yourself on her anyway? How can that be worthwhile?"

"That's what makes it fun," Fowler said. He couldn't keep an ugly leer from his face. Bolan had to restrain himself from punching out the guy right then. If he needed to, he could find the paperwork. It would just take longer.

But then Fowler said, "Here it is." He drew a manila file folder from the drawer and handed it to Bolan. The tab had

IW printed on it in black marker. He looked inside and found records of shipments received and checks cut, and an address in Cleveland of a company called IW Bath.

"Do they deliver it to you, or ship it?"

"They send down a truck," Fowler replied. "We write a check as soon as we've processed the shipment, and put it in the mail."

"You know the principals?"

"Never met them—just my cousin who sets it up," Fowler said. Bolan didn't think he was lying. "The truck driver is usually one of three guys, or sometimes a couple of them together. All my communication with the higher-ups is by phone or email."

Bolan unzipped his bag and started to put the file in it. "You want a copy of that?" Fowler asked.

"No, this is fine."

"But I need that."

"No, you don't," Bolan stated.

"What?"

"You don't need paperwork anymore, because you're going out of the Ivory Wave business," Bolan told him.

"What the hell—"

"Look at it this way," Bolan said. "When I take that file with me, it'll be the one thing that survives the fire."

"Fire? What fi—" A crestfallen look settled on his face. "Listen, I don't know who the hell you are, but this has gone far enough."

"I'm just getting started," Bolan said. He turned his back on the man and started for the door.

He heard the rasp of a desk drawer and spun, dropping the heavy bag and snatching his Beretta 93-R from its shoulder holster. He expected to see a gun in the man's hand, but instead Fowler had drawn a big knife, an ornately etched bowie knife. It was a showpiece, not a serious weapon, but that didn't mean it couldn't do some damage. Fowler charged him, mindless of the gun in Bolan's hand. The soldier holstered the weapon as quickly as he had drawn it, and prepared for the man's attack.

Fowler ran at him, his right hand holding the knife in front of him. Bolan sidestepped the attack, letting the blade slide past him, and caught the arm on either side of the elbow. With the same motion, he pushed up on the man's arm from both sides, snapping the elbow. Fowler shrieked and pulled away, stumbling as he went. As Fowler lurched through the open doorway, his feet looked for traction on the walkway outside, and a pained scream erupted from his lips. His legs got in each other's way and he lost his balance, running into the railing. Bolan started toward him, but too late. The man tumbled over the side, arms pinwheeling, the scream full-throated now, piercing the silence of the warehouse. He hit the floor below with a wet, awful thump.

12

By the time Bolan reached him, Fowler had gasped its last and the sense of urgency to complete the mission was getting stronger.

Bolan didn't feel bad for Fowler. He had helped kill Angela Fulton, and who knew how many others, simply for the sake of his bank account. And the man had meant to kill him. The world was better off without him.

The soldier reached into his bag to begin his real work for the night, placing incendiary devices in locations chosen carefully to inflict maximum damage to the supply of Ivory Wave. But he froze, listening intently, and eased the Beretta from its holster. He sniffed the air, but the smells of Fowler's blood and death covered up anything else. Still, he was convinced he wasn't alone.

"Come on out," he said. "With your hands where I can see them."

Peggy emerged from within the shelving units. "How did you know...?"

"It's just something you do," Bolan said, "if you want to survive. I'm very good at surviving."

She waved toward the corpse of her employer. "You have no idea how many times I've fantasized about something like that," she said. Bolan saw that her lips were parted more than they had been upstairs, where she'd clamped them together anxiously. There was a slight sheen on her forehead and cheeks.

"You really should go," he told her. "What I'm doing here could be dangerous."

"I've already got the impression that you're a dangerous man." Her voice was breathy. "Who are you?"

"Please, Peggy," he said. "You've got to go now. No more questions, no stalling. Just go."

"But—"

"No," he said. "Go. Now."

She looked as if she was going to offer up another argument—or something else—but she saw in his eyes that he meant it. "Whatever," she said. "Just…thanks. For shaking up my world. I needed a kick in the pants, and you gave it to me. Don't worry, I won't say a word—for one thing, I don't want anyone to know I was here when Jed died."

"Thanks," Bolan said.

"By the way, the security cameras record to hard drives stored in that last office." She pointed up the stairs. "You'll want to make sure you deal with those."

"Thanks for that, too."

"And if you change your mind, I…never mind. You look like a man who can figure things out if he wants to. If you change your mind, find me."

"I'll do that," Bolan said. He knew he wouldn't. She might be a fascinating woman, but he didn't have time for her now, and he didn't expect to anytime soon.

This time he watched her until she was actually out the front door. When she was, he went to it and threw the bolt, locking her out. Of course, she might have a key, but he didn't think she'd be back this night.

The next time she did come back, there wouldn't be a warehouse here anymore.

HE STARTED UPSTAIRS, to the room she had pointed out. There were a few computers, and Bolan guessed that the business files were backed up to them, in addition to the security video. He yanked out all the cables and threw the equipment out the door. It sailed over the railing and crashed onto the floor below, shattering on impact. He tossed an armed white phosphorous grenade onto the pile. On his way past Fowler's office, he yanked the pin on an incendiary device and tossed the canister under the manager's desk.

He hurried downstairs. The charge went off with a soft pop and a rush of heat that he could feel before he reached the bottom. It would burn fast, and because the upper floor was close to the roof, the flames would ignite the timbers and tear through the steel and show in the night sky. He didn't have much time to do the rest of what he'd come for.

He rolled the next two canisters under the Ivory Wave section of the warehouse, approaching it from two different angles to make sure he covered it all. Once those went off, he pulled the pins on two more and threw the grenades to the far corners. On his way out the door, he ignited a final one, in order to discourage anyone from rushing in.

Outside, he ran the couple of blocks to the tractor, threw his zippered bag in and climbed up into the seat. Any fire crews would arrive too late, he hoped. When they did arrive, they would find an inferno, and within it, once the fires were contained and extinguished, the broken body of a man.

As long as Peggy kept her mouth shut, nobody would be able to connect Tom Kenner to the fire, and even if they did, they wouldn't be able to connect Mack Bolan to Tom Kenner.

That night, in the motel, Bolan watched a local TV news reporter doing a stand-up outside the "uncontrolled blaze" at the Devilweed warehouse. She tried to keep a straight face, but when she described the products that Devilweed distributed, she almost lost it. When the anchor moved on to a story about a possible cheese shortage at local restaurants, he turned it off and slept.

Send For
2 FREE BOOKS
Today!

I accept your offer!

Please send me two free
novels and a mystery gift (gift
worth about $5). I understand
that these books are completely
free—even the shipping and
handling will be paid—and
I am under no obligation
to purchase anything, ever, as
explained on the back of this card.

366 ADL FVYT   **166 ADL FVYT**

Please Print

FIRST NAME

LAST NAME

ADDRESS

APT.#   CITY

STATE/PROV.   ZIP/POSTAL CODE

Visit us online at
www.ReaderService.com

Offer limited to one per household and not applicable to series that subscriber is currently receiving.

Your Privacy—The Harlequin® Reader Service is committed to protecting your privacy. Our Privacy Policy is available
online at www.ReaderService.com or upon request from the Harlequin Reader Service. We make a portion of our
mailing list available to reputable third parties that offer products we believe may interest you. If you prefer that we
not exchange your name with third parties, or if you wish to clarify or modify your communication preferences, please
visit us at www.ReaderService.com/consumerschoice or write to us at Harlequin Reader Service Preference Service,
P.O. Box 9062, Buffalo, NY 14269. Include your complete name and address.

© 2012 WORLDWIDE LIBRARY® and ™ are trademarks owned and used by the trademark owner and/or its licensee. Printed in the U.S.A. ▶ Detach card and mail today. No stamp needed. ▶ GE-GF-13

13

Massimo Chiarello sat in the conference room at the NDC Consolidated Industries building, listening to his father chairing a meeting unlike any other that had taken place in this room. Large windows on the end of the room faced toward Lake Erie, though buildings between there and the lake obstructed the view, except from the upper floors. Nuncio stood at the front of the room, pacing back and forth in front of a whiteboard that had been rolled in for the meeting.

There were fourteen men in the room, men who had worked for Nuncio for years and years and had demonstrated their loyalty and their courage time and again. Most of them had been with Nuncio since the old days. They had beaten shopkeepers with baseball bats and sawed-off pool cues for Nuncio. They had capped people, cut off heads and hands and dumped bodies into the lake or buried them under construction projects. One of them, Marco Cosimo, had been with Nuncio the day his wife was buried; he was the man who drove Nuncio home from the funeral and served as Nuncio's crutch until he was able to get his feet back under him.

Massimo didn't like all the talk of war, because he felt as if he was at war with himself. He knew that he was the single individual most responsible for the entire mess. Nuncio had been pushed over the edge by the scene at his Shaker Heights house. He was convinced there was a major attack coming on him and his interests, and he wasn't wrong about that. But he didn't know that his own son, the man sitting at the far end of the table, was the point man in that assault.

If he ever found out, Massimo was dead. If his father didn't kill him, Gino would. Gino idolized the old man, worshipped the ground he walked on. He loved the fact that Nuncio held on to the appearance of going straight. Finding legal substances and making them more powerful was easier than evading the police for illegal drugs. The best part was, if the operation was shut down they could feign ignorance with the cops and shunt the enterprise into other kinds of products. He enjoyed the hustle of the business world. But if Nuncio had wanted to stay—like Uncle Dom—an old-line gangster, Gino would have gone along with that, too, though not as happily. Where Massimo had a mean streak, Gino was soft. Massimo was huge, Gino slight. He took after their father, while Massimo had always been more like their mother. She'd had a spine of steel until cancer racked her body from the inside out.

So he sat at the table and listened to the conversation, but his head was spinning with the knowledge that *he* was the enemy under discussion. He tried to look engaged and involved, but he was sweating rivers under his T-shirt and tracksuit.

"At Brendan's suggestion, I brought in the cops," Nuncio was saying. "Acting all innocent and everything."

"It wasn't acting," Brendan said. "You didn't do anything wrong."

Nuncio took a long drag on his cigar, illuminating the tip like a beacon. "Right. Anyway, they took the place apart. Crime scene techs, photographs, video, everything. They spent pretty much the whole day there. They'll have records of everybody who's been in and out of the house. That sucks, but we haven't used it for anything illegal. Only problem will be if we do need to exact some kind of retribution, then we've brought attention to ourselves, and they'll have our fingerprints and all on the record."

"That's true," Gino said. "But it doesn't matter. We have to take action."

Nuncio rubbed the ever-growing bald area above his forehead. "Yeah, you're right. We let somebody do that to us and we don't strike back, we're finished. Every second-rate punk in the Midwest will come in here and walk all over us."

"We won't let that happen, Papa," Gino said. "We'll find out who it was and we'll do them double, no matter what."

"It won't be easy," Nuncio said. "And it might be risky. But you're right, we will do it. You're all working your contacts, right? See if there's anybody out on the street talking about the hit. Thing like that, people brag. All we need is for one idiot to mouth off and we'll have them. Soon as you hear anything, any of you, let me know. Day or night, anytime. We can't sit on it once we find out."

"What other steps are you taking, Nunce?" Gordon Hawkins asked. He was one of NDC's various vice presidents, a man who had come from the business community rather than the crime community, and had made himself invaluable.

"Such as?"

"Listening around is all good and well, but you could be taking more direct action, too," Hawkins stated. "There are a limited number of outfits that would even try something like this, right? It has to be somebody local, for starters, to have known about the game. So snatch up somebody from each operation you think could be involved and work them until you get answers. Put out the word that there'll be a reward for anybody who turns in the hitters, and make it a big one. For five million bucks, most people would betray their own mother."

Massimo saw his father thinking over that suggestion. He didn't believe the man could put together five million in cash very quickly. But Hawkins was right—Dario would rat him out for a quarter of that. Hell, he'd do it for ten grand and a half-hour head start getting out of town.

Maybe Massimo should take out the other guys who were there, Nico, Dario and Artie. Not Uncle Dom. He was a hard case who wouldn't break. And maybe Nico would be okay. He had been with Uncle Dom in the joint; he didn't owe any long-term loyalty to Nuncio. But Dario and Artie were already taking a chance by moving against their boss. They might see some sort of salvation in confession.

It would be easiest to take Dario and Artie out *before* they heard about any reward. After, they might get more careful.

Massimo couldn't ever forget that he had been the one who pulled the trigger. For that reason, the others couldn't be trusted. Not completely.

"I have another question, Nunce," Marco Cosimo said. He was a distinguished-looking man, with silver hair swept back from his forehead and a lean, patrician face. Massimo had always thought he looked like a college professor. Or at least someone who played a college professor in the movies, which was as close as Massimo had ever been to one.

"What is it?"

"Where's your brother Dominic in all this? Shouldn't he be here?"

"Yeah," Brendan said. "Dom's badass. He can help out."

Massimo's stomach lurched. He had been silently hoping that nobody mentioned Uncle Dom.

"My brother needs more time to adjust to being on the outside," Nuncio said. "He was away for a long time. Since he got back, he's been…well, distant. He's only been here once, and he's never set foot in the office I gave him. He's got to figure out what his involvement in the business will be, and we'll go from there. I haven't talked to him yet about what happened at the house, but I will after we're done here."

Cosimo nodded, as if satisfied by Nuncio's answer. Massimo wouldn't have been. Why haven't you told him, he would have asked. Don't you think he's got exactly the kind of experience we need here? We've been legitimate businessmen for more than a decade, and now we're supposed to just set that aside and go back to our old ways. We could use someone on our side who never gave up the life.

But he was glad that Cosimo didn't press. He would call Uncle Dom as soon as he could, and warn him that Nuncio would be checking in.

Then he would figure out a way to get rid of Artie, Dario and Nico. He was sure Uncle Dom would understand. Those guys could get him and Uncle Dom killed or arrested. Either fate had to be avoided. If Uncle Dom went back inside, he would never come out.

And Massimo *had* to remain free. He had found a new hobby, a new passion. Killing those guys would solve two problems at once—it would protect him and Uncle Dom, and it would allow him to practice the thing he now loved more than anything else in the world.

"One more thing has just come up tonight," Nuncio said. "Most of you haven't heard about this yet. I don't know if it's related, but I feel like it must be. Somebody hit our distribution center in Fort Wayne tonight. Burned it to the ground. I just got the call right before I came in here, and I'm still waiting to find out the extent of the damage. But we had a lot of product sitting there, and my understanding is that it's gone. A total loss."

"Fort Wayne?" somebody echoed.

"That's right."

"How the hell does somebody hit us here and in Fort Wayne both?" Cosimo asked.

"If I knew that, I would have made sure it didn't happen. Anyway, the place there isn't ours, *per se*. They ship for us, but it's strictly a buy-sell relationship. Artie's cousin helped us set it up. It's just the timing makes me wonder. I've learned there's no such thing as coincidence. And of course we'll have to make up the loss somewhere, because there will be costs associated with this other thing. Let's talk to our chemist friend—he had other ideas about products that could be laced."

AFTER HE TALKED to his uncle Dom, Massimo called Dario. "Where are you, man?" he asked.

"At my crib, getting ready for bed."

"Dude, it's only, what?"

"Massimo, it's almost one o'clock. I work tomorrow."

"So do I. Listen, man, we gotta talk. I thought maybe we'd go to a club, see some naked chicks, grab a beer. What do you think?" Dario was a handsome guy, had grown up getting all the pussy he could handle, Massimo knew, but he was always on the lookout for more. Pussy, Massimo had told him many times, would be the death of him. Dario's answer was always the same: "What a way to go, though."

"I don't want to leave the house."

"I just came from a meeting that Papa had. About that poker game."

"I didn't hear about it," Dario replied.

"High-level only," Massimo said. "No soldiers. You'll hear about it from your *capo*."

"So it's like that? Your dad's going back to those old ways?"

"Sometimes the old ways are the best ways. Look, I don't want to talk about this stuff over the phone. I'll come over in about twenty minutes. We'll go out someplace and I'll tell you what's up."

"Okay," Dario finally agreed. "I'll get dressed and see you in a few."

Fifteen minutes later, Massimo pulled up outside Dario's place. He wasn't going to honk the horn, but then he did anyway. He was wired, as if all the blood in his body was shooting through his veins at ten times the normal speed. He wasn't on anything except caffeine and adrenaline, but they were enough. He had raced over here, sixty on residential streets, fifty through a business district. All the cops in Cleveland were either in for the night or glomming doughnuts in some other neighborhood, so he made it without trouble. But as he waited for Dario, he was tapping his feet on the pedals and drumming his fingers on the wheel and moving his ass in the seat, and the only music was in his head, and the only lyric he heard was *kill kill kill kill kill.*

Finally Dario came out. He wore a leather jacket over a dark T-shirt, jeans and black leather running shoes. He got in on the passenger side and buckled his seat belt. He was always a cautious one, Dario. They tapped fists.

"Where you wanna go?" Dario asked.

"Someplace we can get some boobs in our face," Massimo said. He cranked the engine. The stereo blared hip-hop, and he turned it down, then put the car in gear.

"So what happened at the meeting? Who was there?"

Massimo filled him in. He told his friend everything— how he had felt knowing everybody in the room was talking about him, about the suggestions—snatching up members of other local criminal organizations and torturing them until they spilled. About the reward.

Dario gave a low whistle. "Five million bucks?"

"There's no way Papa can put that together," Massimo said. "Not right away. I mean, he's got it, but it's not all cash." He pulled the car over to the curb. He had been driving down quiet suburban streets, most of the houses dark. Where he stopped, he was under the sweeping branches of a willow tree that blocked most of the light from the street lamps along the sidewalk.

"We picking someone else up?" Dario asked. "This don't look like no strip club."

"Yeah," Massimo said. He pointed toward the nearest house, which he had never seen in his life. "She lives there."

"She?"

"She's a wild one, loves giving lap dances. Come on, let's go get her."

"Both of us?"

"Maybe we'll never make it to the club." Massimo grabbed his door handle, opened his door an inch or so. At the same time, Dario opened his door.

As soon as Dario's back was turned, Massimo looped a powerful arm around his neck from behind. Dario's reaction was slow, as if he thought at first that the move was a playful one. "Sorry about this, bud," Massimo said.

In a way, he really was. He had always kind of liked Dario.

But killing someone with his bare hands was something he hadn't tried yet, and he'd been itching to do it. He grabbed his right arm with his left hand, cinching it tighter over Dario's throat. The other man was struggling now, punching Massimo's arm, kicking, trying to get out of the car. But Massimo had sixty pounds on him, and it was solid muscle. Dario couldn't budge him, or break his grip.

Dario tried to change tactics. He clawed at the .45 he kept in a shoulder rig. Massimo had anticipated the move, and he released his own right arm and jabbed his left thumb into Dario's left eye. He felt something give under the sudden pressure, and Dario let out a choking cry of agony. His hands went to his face, the gun forgotten, and Massimo snaked it from the holster before he could remember. He dropped it on the floor at his feet.

Dario's kicking was becoming more urgent, but Massimo

was having an easier time holding him in the car. He knew his friend was fading. Before the end, he released Dario and gave him a push.

The man sputtered and choked and fell from the car. Massimo got out then, and walked around the vehicle. He found Dario on the other side, struggling to get to his hands and knees. He was barely able to lift his head to see his attacker, and when he did his face was purple and blotchy. Bright red blood flecked the corners of his mouth, and his left eye was seeping.

He tried to say something, but got out only a croaking noise. Massimo took a step toward him, then another, then, without breaking stride, drew back his right foot and aimed a vicious kick at Dario's head.

His boot caught his friend in the cheekbone. Massimo felt it give under the blow, and Dario's head flew sideways. He collapsed in the grass between the curb and sidewalk. Massimo kicked him again, three times, each time feeling Dario's skull coming apart, his head taking on an almost jellylike consistency. Finally Massimo stood right next to the other man, raised his knee chest-high and brought his foot down on the pulpy mass that had been the back of Dario's head.

"Not so handsome anymore, are you?" he asked.

The corpse didn't answer.

Lights were starting to flicker on in the nearest couple of houses. Massimo got back into the car and closed his own door, and relied on centrifugal force from his sudden acceleration to close the other.

That, he thought as he raced away, was awesome!

14

Bolan left the trailer parked behind the motel when he checked out in the morning. At some point, the motel's owner would figure out that it had been abandoned there, and didn't belong to any continuing guests. He didn't mind driving the tractor—it was less discreet than he liked, but it had plenty of power and it gave him a good, elevated view of the road.

He had an address in the Cleveland, Ohio, area for the manufacturer of Ivory Wave—the IW Labs printed on the packaging. According to the paperwork he had taken from Fowler, IW Labs was really a company called IW Bath. And according to Stony Man Farm, nobody was yet looking for the truck—but then, it would be a while, if ever, before Devilweed Inc. was organized enough to realize that one was missing. The bigger question might be what the other drivers would do with their trucks. Presumably, since the fire and then Fowler's death had been all over the news, both last night and this morning, they had all heard that their boss and their home base were gone.

The morning was bright and clear. It was the kind of morning when it would almost be possible to look around and think the world was a joyful, peaceful place. One could almost believe that one's fellow citizens, one's fellow human beings were good, honest people who cared for one another.

And to a certain extent, Bolan knew that was true. A soldier could never forget that most people weren't combatants but innocents. Sometimes they were caught in a cross fire, and sometimes circumstances swept them into battle. He had become used to the idea that he would always be a combatant, and that protecting the innocent would always be part of his mission.

Another part of it, though, would remain identifying and eliminating the enemy. It was the only way for the small parts of the world to stay safe. That's what Bolan had on his mind as he drove through the Midwestern daylight, hitting a brief, sun-drenched shower near Beaverdam.

CLEVELAND WAS THE home of the Rock and Roll Hall of Fame, and an old rock song called "Look Out Cleveland" came into his mind as he neared the city. The song warned of a storm coming, and Bolan knew there was indeed a storm approaching the city. Only, this storm was the Executioner, and no amount of preparation could aid those whom the storm would target.

By afternoon, he had located the address from Fowler's files.

He drove past it once, taking in as much as he could from behind the wheel. It was a roadside building that could have once been a large restaurant or a supermarket, wood framed and with an old, peeling-shingle roof. The windows had been boarded over and graffiti decorated the boards. The paint had probably been a rich brown once, but it had faded to a dull, dirty gray. The parking area was choked with weeds. Most people would drive right by, thinking it was a vacant building in a strip where there were plenty of them spaced widely apart. At the intersection there was a clutch of fast-food restaurants and gas stations, but after that the businesses appeared to be less profitable—a low-budget furniture store,

a junkyard, a carpet warehouse, with lots of empties in between.

But Mack Bolan wasn't most people.

He saw that the driveway on the east side of the building—
to the right of it, from his angle—was worn smoother than
the other. The weeds there were shorter, and confined to the
center of the path. Where the wheels of vehicles would go,
there were tracks that were worn clear of growth, and they
led all the way around the building to what was presumably
a parking area in back. Behind that was a twelve-foot chain-
link fence, with slats woven in so tightly that a person would
have to be right up against it to see through. The fence was
topped with coils of razor wire.

And he saw more. In the shadows of the eaves, at three
points across the span of the building's front, were dark boxes
that he suspected held cameras. A little run-down trailer
was parked behind the genuinely vacant business next door.
Across the street sat an old Dodge with paint that had oxi-
dized and turned white, with two men sitting quietly inside it.

He took all that in as he cruised past, a few miles per hour
below the speed limit but not slow enough, he hoped, to attract attention. There were no nearby blocks, no intersection
he could turn down, for more than a mile. Even when he did,
there wouldn't be another parallel road running right past the
back of the property.

Instead, Bolan found a motel a couple of blocks away,
checked in and parked the truck in back. In the room, he
turned on the air-conditioning and his laptop. He called up a
satellite view of the area and zoomed in on the structure as
closely as he could get. When he pushed way in, the image
blurred, so he got in touch with Stony Man. Twenty minutes
later, after a nearby satellite had been slightly repurposed, he
had a far crisper image—and of the way the building looked
right now, not two years earlier.

He had been right about a few things. The parking area behind the building was indeed cleaner and better maintained than the spaces visible from the street. The tall fence surrounded a field, a long shack occupying a corner, with a pickup truck parked beside it. Another pickup truck and a couple of garbage cans were behind the trailer on the property next door.

An empty trailer didn't need garbage cans.

What had looked like a vacant storefront was in fact being watched from a variety of angles. It was remotely possible that the observers were law enforcement, but Bolan didn't think so. He was familiar with law enforcement, even with undercover officers, and he didn't get the impression that the people he had seen in the Dodge were cops.

Instead, he thought he was looking at a carefully planned defensive force. No doubt there were people inside the building who could also provide protection, but he suspected that most people who tried to get into the building without authorization would be stopped well before they reached the front door. There was apparently enough money in the Ivory Wave business to cover a reasonably large payroll.

The light was draining from the day as Bolan walked across the parking lot to a nearby coffee shop. There were stools available at the counter, and booths alongside the window. A waitress in a red uniform with a stained white apron caught his eye as he walked in. "Sit anywhere, honey," she said. Her hair was coppery, cut just off her shoulder, and her lipstick was as bright red as her dress.

He took one of the booths and pulled a menu from a holder at the end of the table. There was nothing surprising on it. He considered a steak, but decided the burger would be a safer bet. He added a salad and some green vegetables. "And coffee," he said. "Just bring the pot."

"Staying up late?" the waitress asked. The name badge on

her breast identified her as Rhonda. She was in her mid-thirties, he guessed, and she looked like someone life had thrown a lot of curveballs at. But she had laugh lines at the corners of her mouth and around her eyes, and she moved with a brisk efficiency that Bolan found appealing.

"Only if I have to," he told her.

"Working tonight?"

"Most nights, it seems like."

"Doing what?"

"A little of this, a little of that."

She graced him with a smile that was surprisingly infectious. "A man of mystery," she said. "I like that."

"I've been called worse," he said.

She took his order to the kitchen and came back with his pot of coffee, fresh and steaming. She poured the first cup, tossed him another smile, then went to the cash register to check out another customer. She and a single cook appeared to be running the place alone.

Just the same, it was quiet enough that she stopped by his table often, to check on him or just to chat. Most of the people in the restaurant were travelers: a family with two tired kids, three truckers who obviously had known one another long enough to be comfortable sitting in near silence, sipping coffee or sodas and chewing their food thoughtfully.

When Rhonda wasn't visiting, Bolan was running through approach scenarios in his mind. He could surveil the building for long enough to find out when the shifts changed. Chances were, the various watchers would interact, nodding or even speaking to those they had been standing guard with, and those replacing them. In that way, he could get a sense of their capabilities, even their ordnance.

But he had no idea what kind of schedule they were on, so it might take a solid twenty-four hours of watching the watchers to learn their time line. And he would have to remain unobserved the whole time. He could get some intel from the satellite, but that wouldn't help with the close-up part. It wouldn't let him make his own judgments about how the men handled themselves. The way a man walked to his car and got in could tell a trained observer a lot. The way he drove the car. The way he got out of it and walked into a building. The way a man moved said a lot about whether he could handle himself, and Bolan knew that if he was going to go that route, he would want to watch the men for himself, get to know them.

There was another option, though. More direct. Possibly more risky.

That didn't particularly bother him.

15

Bolan made a couple of educated guesses about what was going on inside the seemingly empty building that housed the Ivory Wave manufacturing facility, even though he had never been inside. The first was that they would be busy this night. They were panicked—they had lost a major distributor of their product. Maybe more significantly, they had lost all the product already stored at the Devilweed warehouse. He had only a single file detailing the most recent couple of transactions, so the paperwork hadn't made clear how much of the product had been paid for. If Devilweed was like most distribution companies, they held off paying as long as they could, so that they had money coming in from the retailers before they had to compensate the suppliers.

They would be putting in extra hours, trying to manufacture enough "bath salts" to maintain their cash flow.

The other thing he knew was that they wouldn't be at their best, mentally or physically. Even people who typically worked nights experienced a stretch in the middle of the night when their circadian rhythms protested the hour, usually around three in the morning. If, as he believed, the destruction of the Devilweed warehouse had these people putting in extra shifts, then some of those working wouldn't be accustomed to the hours. Besides the workers simply not performing at full capacity, the place would be more crowded than usual, and some of the sleepy ones would be getting in the way of the rest. It was, Bolan believed, possibly a less productive night than it would have been if they had just run a regular shift. But panic pushed people into making some bad decisions.

He was hoping to have his own impact on their productivity.

Dressed in his blacksuit, wearing his favorite weapons and with additional ordnance in the zippered bag open on the seat next to him, Bolan drove the tractor back to the IW building. As he approached, he noticed that there was still a car parked across the street with two men in it, but not the Dodge he had seen before. He suspected the other security precautions he had seen remained in place. He had considered, and rejected, various ways to circumvent them.

And he had settled on the most direct approach.

He tugged on a Kevlar balaclava and situated it for maximum visibility. As he neared the building, he pressed down on the accelerator and worked the gears. Maintaining speed and making the turn would require a tricky balance, especially in a tractor in which he hadn't tried anything quite so complicated. At the last moment he braked and cranked the wheel. The tractor responded, slower to make the turn than he had hoped, but he corrected and steered toward the ramshackle wooden building. When he was confident of his course, he braked again, slowing only slightly, and braced for impact.

The tractor's nose plowed into the building's facade with a tremendous crash, splintering wood and crunching steel. As the windshield spiderwebbed and shattered, Bolan saw a wooden beam snap and copper pipes torn loose from their moorings. Glass and shredded wood hit him, snagging against his Kevlar vest and headgear, but he protected his face with his arms and avoided the worst of it.

Inside was chaos.

The tractor came to rest, water and oil dripping from its undercarriage, in a laboratory-like space. If the place had been as clean as a commercial lab before, which Bolan doubted, it wasn't after most of the front wall had been pushed into it. The staff was mostly male, though there were a few women, maybe thirty people in all. They were standing in horror or crouched or seeking refuge from the snorting steel monster that had appeared in their midst. Some were screaming, others silent.

Interior walls had been torn down, so the operation largely took place in one big room. The owners probably didn't trust their workers and wanted everyone to be able to keep an eye on everyone else. The place looked like a cross between a high school chemistry lab and a small-time candy factory. It had workbenches for combining products stored in large bins, equipment for processing the mixtures, for packing it into envelopes or capsules, and for packaging those into the little cartons Bolan had first seen at Flat Water Smokes-n-Stuff. Against one wall was a row of doors, most of them closed, with curtained windows. Offices, he guessed. All of it was lit by banks of overhead fluorescents hanging from the ceiling, but one bank had gone out entirely, and the lights of another were flickering.

Bolan wrenched open the driver's door and slid from his seat with his ordnance bag in hand. Mixed in among the lab workers was a handful of armed men, present no doubt to keep the help honest as much as to deal with any potential intruders. One of them lifted a shotgun to his shoulder and sighted on the truck. Bolan squeezed off a triple burst from his M-16 and tore three holes in the man's throat and skull, spraying the wall behind him with blood. A second gunner had been trapped against a wall by a workbench that had fallen over when Bolan crashed in, but he managed to get a submachine gun pointed. The Executioner turned the M-16 on him, blowing the back of his head off.

Someone got off a shot that pinged against the truck's grille. Bolan ducked behind some wreckage as the next shot came closer. This time, he was able to isolate the source: a young man, barely out of his teens, with long hair and a bushy mustache. He had a 9 mm semiautomatic pistol, but he was firing it single-shot, and he projected an air of confidence. He was lining up his next shot when Bolan emerged from cover and squeezed off three shots that hit him in the center of the chest, carrying him back a couple of feet before dropping him on the ground.

One of the employees—he looked like a lab worker, in a white coat that was stained and dirty—charged Bolan with a long, wicked shard of glass in his hand. The soldier spun the M-16 and slammed the stock into his attacker's gut. The man huffed and doubled over, his fist instinctively squeezing the glass. Then he screamed as it bit into his hand. Bolan smashed a big fist into the man's face and he went down.

The rest of the people surrounding the soldier appeared to be lab workers. None made a move toward him. The air was still full of dust and smoke, and the sounds of people shuffling around, sobbing and crying out in pain almost masked the noise of others approaching—the guards who had been posted outside the building.

Bolan moved deeper into the structure. Workers parted for him, or ran as he approached. At this point he had little worry about them attacking him, but the outside guards would want to make up for their inability to prevent his entry.

He ducked behind a workbench in one of the darker sections of the room. He didn't doubt that someone would point out his location, but at least the solid wooden bench would help shield him. There were several now between him and the toppled section of wall. Men were shouting, some demanding to know where the attacker was, others simply giving the kinds of adrenaline-jacking yells common to males with their blood up.

To enhance the general confusion, Bolan reached into his bag and pulled out three smoke grenades. He yanked the pins and threw the bombs in different directions, clouding the air with mustard-colored smoke. Somebody shot in his direction, but he hadn't shown himself above the workbench, and the slugs went wide of their mark.

The next grenade Bolan pulled wasn't a smoker. He had identified the part of the lab where the raw materials were stored, boxes upon boxes of them. He tugged the pin free and hurled the grenade in that direction. He heard it clunk against the wall, then the floor. Somebody screeched in terror, then the bomb blew with a boom that echoed off the remaining walls.

More gunfire. They were getting his location by watching where the grenades were coming from.

He would have done the same thing in their position.

The thing was, he was narrowing down their locations, too.

One of them was using the tractor's door for cover. Bolan thought there was a second one close to him, maybe standing behind the vehicle and coming out only to fire. He armed and tossed a grenade in that direction. It bounced off the ruined hood. He could hear someone scrambling on the slippery tile floor, trying to pick it up. But then it blew and the man's cry was cut off by the explosion. Bolan tucked himself into a tight ball, his mouth open and his hands clamped over his ears. An instant later, the truck's gas tank blew. The soldier could feel the wave of heat spreading through the building, accompanied by the thick smell of burning fuel and renewed screams from the employees who hadn't yet scattered.

When Bolan looked again, he saw the vehicle engulfed in flames. Because it had come to a halt enmeshed in the debris from the wooden wall, the wood had already caught, and fire rushed toward the ceiling. The building had an automatic sprinkler system installed, but it hadn't come on. Either he had disrupted it by driving through the wall, or it had been disconnected sometime in the past. Maybe it had been installed by whatever business had preceded the drug lab in the space, and then left up for show.

He saw a couple more guys coming in through a back door, guns blazing wildly into the smoke. He didn't wait for them to get their bearings, but raised the M-16 and unleashed a couple of triburts, cutting them down there they stood.

Bolan made a quick visual sweep of the room. He couldn't see any more combatants. Those who had been inside when he crashed through had left in ones and twos, and now the rest were heading for the exits, both those that had existed before and the new one he had made—though anyone leaving that way had to pass uncomfortably close to what was becoming a conflagration.

He grabbed a guy who came within reach. "Who's in charge of this place?" he demanded.

The guy shot him a blank look. Panic had wiped his mind. Bolan shook him. "Where's your boss?" Finally understanding dawned, and the guy pointed toward the row of offices.

Looking at them again, Bolan saw an uneven glow behind the curtains in one window. He released the man, snatched up his bag and raced in that direction, ignoring those who rushed past him. They were just people doing what they had to in order to make it from one paycheck to the next. Killing them would serve no purpose.

When he reached the office he tried the doorknob, but it wouldn't turn. He reared back and gave it a snap-kick, next to the knob. The door buckled and the jamb splintered, and the door swung open, half torn off its upper hinge.

Inside, a man stood beside a small floor safe with its door

open, throwing documents into a flaming metal wastebasket. He was a white guy with thinning brown hair combed back from his face, and he was wearing plastic-rimmed glasses, a pale blue short-sleeved shirt, khaki pants and an expression of terror. He was drenched in sweat.

"Stop what you're doing," Bolan commanded.

The guy had an armful of files. He froze.

"Drop them on the desk," Bolan said. He was still carrying the M-16 and the open bag, but he hadn't pointed a weapon at the man. His presence was all he needed.

The man did as he was told. The look on his face was one of utter defeat. Bolan realized he was only a lab rat, put into a position of authority over this operation. But he was no tough guy, no gangster.

He relaxed his stance, leaning against the doorjamb. "There's no need to keep feeding that fire," he told the man. "This whole place is burning down."

"The fire at Devilweed?" the man said. "That was…"

"I guess it's becoming a habit," Bolan said. "You're the boss here, right?"

"Yeah," the guy said. He sounded both afraid and resigned. "Yeah, that's me. I mean, on this end. Production."

"There's another end?" Bolan asked.

The man shook his head. "Don't even ask."

"I'm asking. Nicely, this time."

"What are you going to do if I don't answer? Torture me?"

Bolan shrugged. "If I have to."

"You might as well get started, then." The man looked into the dying flames in the wastebasket. From the big room outside, Bolan could hear the crackle of the much larger fire. He didn't have much time to wrap this up, not if he hoped to get out alive. "I don't know who you are or why you're here. And I'm not a brave man, by any means. But I'm a loyal man, and the people who employed me to run this place took a chance on me that nobody else would take. I'll be damned if I'm going to betray their trust."

"Took a chance?" Bolan asked, curious in spite of the urgency.

"I did some things," the man said. "Doesn't matter what. I shouldn't have, but I did. I spent some time in prison for it. And let me tell you, that's no picnic. When I came out, I didn't think I'd ever work in my field again. But...somebody hired me, I'm not saying who. And while this might not be the most noble use of my talents, it's profitable, and I understand that many people enjoy the product we manufacture here. So I'll say it again, torture me if you must, but don't expect me to say anything."

Bolan couldn't bring himself to like the man, but he at least respected his honesty and forthrightness. He couldn't fault a man for wanting to be loyal to someone who had given him a much-needed break. Too bad that loyalty had come at the price of Angela's life.

"I can't leave you here. You'll be coming in with me," Bolan said. Sweat was pooling under his balaclava.

"I guess I understand that." He paused for a long moment, then continued. "Can you give me a minute?"

"Give me your phone," Bolan said.

"My phone?"

"Your cell." He wouldn't need the man if he had that, and once he turned him over to the police there was no way he'd get the information he wanted.

The man looked as if he might object, then thought better of it. He probably realized that Bolan could just wait and then take it. He fished in his right hip pocket, pulled out a smartphone and held it out.

Bolan stepped forward and took it. "Is there anyone you want to call? You may not get a chance once the police get hold of you," he asked.

The man didn't even think about it. "No. There's no one. Not anymore."

"Okay."

The fire in the wastebasket had dwindled to embers. Bolan kicked over the can, scattering the ashes, and left the office. Outside, the lab was empty. Flames had run across the ceiling and spread out from the truck. Bolan couldn't wait much longer without being here when the firefighters showed up. He wanted to drop off the chemist at the local police department and be on his way. He was beginning to wonder if he had made a mistake, leaving the man alone in his office, but then he heard the crack of a single gunshot.

He hurried back in. The man was sitting in his desk chair, his head tilted back. There was a quarter-sized hole in the back of his skull, and droplets of blood spattered the ceiling. His hands were limp at his sides. The soldier took the formulas the chemist had been using and left the building.

16

The ringing phone woke Nuncio.

He sat up in bed and grabbed it. The TV was on. It was a habit he had fallen into after his wife's death—he could no longer fall asleep without its sound and light filling the room. He snatched up the remote and pressed the mute button. "Yeah?"

Nuncio listened to a panic-stricken voice on the other end, Gordon Hawkins. Once he would have used the word *capo* to describe Gordon's role in the organization, and the more he heard, the more he thought it would come to that again. And soon.

When Gordon had filled him in, he hung up the phone and swore. It wasn't even seven-thirty yet, and he liked to sleep until eight. But he wasn't going back to sleep now. He wasn't sure he would ever get to sleep again.

He paced for a minute, then returned to the phone and called Marco Cosimo. "The Ivory Wave lab was hit last night," he said.

"I know," Cosimo replied. "It's on the morning news."

"Why didn't you tell me? I had to hear it from Gordo."

"I figured you knew."

"Fuck!" Nuncio exploded. "First the house, then the distributor and now this! Who the hell is trying to kill me?"

"Nunce," Cosimo said, "if whoever was doing all this wanted you dead, I think you'd already be dead."

"Yeah, maybe. But still, it's all getting closer and closer. We've got to do something."

"You got something in mind?"

"More of what we're already doing. Shaking the trees to see if anything falls out. But we need to think about defensive measures, too. I have to be safe enough to function. And we need to keep senior staff protected."

"Definitely," Cosimo agreed. "Everybody might have to hole up somewhere. Your place, or the office building?"

"Let me think about it," Nuncio said. "Both have advantages. We can handle more people at the building, and still keep business running. Whatever's left of it. But home will be more comfortable, if we're in for a long siege."

"You remember what they used to call it," Cosimo said. "Going to the mattresses."

"Right."

"If we need to, we can bring mattresses to the building. Whatever it takes, Nunce. We got to put a stop to this and we got to do it fast."

"You don't have to tell me that," Nuncio said. He would never admit it to any of his people, but he was getting scared.

He was old, by some standards. Certainly older than a lot of his predecessors ever lived to. Luciano, the guy he'd looked up to most, the guy he considered his spiritual godfather for the way he'd applied business methodology to the rackets, had made it to the age of sixty-four. Capone, forty-eight. Bugsy Siegel, forty-one. Albert Anastasia, fifty-five. Joe Gallo had died on his forty-third birthday. Those with shorter life spans had usually died at the hands of others. Everyone in the life remembered the story of Anastasia's murder, sitting in a barber chair when two soldiers started shooting at him. Anastasia was tough enough to come out of the chair at them, but he charged their reflection in the mirror instead of the shooters, and he died in a pool of his own blood.

Nobody ever said the life was safe. But part of Nuncio's rationale for taking things into more legit areas was to make it safer. He wanted to watch his grandchildren grow up, and he wanted to die peacefully in his own damn bed with the TV on. Watching his brother go to prison had been scary; imagining his own bloody death was more so.

"Listen," he told Cosimo, "I'll meet you in the office later and we'll come up with a plan. In the meantime, don't trust a fucking soul. All I know, your wife could be putting rat poison in that famous Bolognese sauce of hers."

"I'll be there, Nunce," Cosimo said. "You watch your back."

ACROSS TOWN, DOMINIC CHIARELLO sat in a café with Artie D'Amato. There were no other customers in the place. The barista was a hooker Artie had known for years, who had wanted to get out of the business after a client had sliced a three-inch gash down her cheek. Artie hadn't wanted a scarred woman pouring him coffee, so he had paid for plastic surgery, throwing in breast implants at the same time, and employed her to run the shop. She could be counted on to keep her mouth shut. Just the same, the men spoke in low voices. The morning customers had been chased away and Massimo loomed in the doorway to discourage newcomers.

"Dario was a good kid," Artie said. His eyes were liquid; Chiarello was afraid he would start crying. There was nothing wrong with spilling a tear for a fallen soldier, but Artie had a tendency toward blubbery weeping. It was, Chiarello thought, unseemly. "Kind of a pussy hound, but a good kid just the same. Loyal as hell, too."

"I know," Chiarello said. Loyal to Artie and therefore to him, but not, Chiarello assumed, loyal to Nuncio, or he wouldn't have thrown in with them so easily when Dominic decided to break with his brother. "You got any ideas? Anybody pissed at him?"

"Not that I know about. If Nunce found out…"

"If Nunce found out, he would have come after me first, not Dario. Me, then you, that's the order it would go. Dario's way down the food chain."

"You're probably right."

No "probably" about it, Chiarello thought. He left it unsaid, though. The man was grieving. Not an appropriate time to argue about trivialities.

"On the other hand…"

"What, Dom?"

Chiarello hadn't seen the body himself. Somebody in the neighborhood had found it and reported it to the police. Dario's wallet had been gone, but his fingers were intact, and they had his prints on file. They had run those and learned the mangled corpse's identity. A detective had called Dario's mother, who had been unwilling to identify the body. But she had called Artie, and he had taken care of that no doubt unpleasant task. From what he had described to Dominic, the kid had looked as if he'd been dragged around the city from the axle of a garbage truck, and run over a few times for good measure.

"You said he was really beat up."

"As bad as I've ever seen. Just had the shit kicked out of him, and then some."

"Like, tortured?" Chiarello asked.

"Could be, I guess."

"What do you think?"

"I don't know, Dom. One thing, though. If he *was* tortured, given the condition he was in when I saw him, he probably talked. I don't know how you could take that kind of punishment without talking. But there wasn't any finesse to it, just pure destruction. Demolition—the kid was demolished. That handsome face was just gone."

"So it could be that my brother caught wind of something but wasn't sure enough to come after us. But now he or his people have had a conversation with Dario. Which means now they are sure, and we're next on the list."

Artie nodded. His face was as pale as Chiarello had ever seen it. "That's possible, sure."

"Seems more than just possible to me. I don't know how they got on to the kid, but if we don't do something fast, we're dead men."

"What do we do?"

"We could hole up in a cave somewhere," Chiarello suggested. "But I'd rather take the fight to them."

"You want to go up against your own brother?"

"He's been legit for a while now, right? I'm betting he's gotten soft. But I haven't. Have you?"

"Tell you the truth, Dom," Artie said, "it's been a while since I've had to get violent with anybody."

"We'll bring in some out-of-town muscle," Chiarello said. "But we've got to move fast. Before anybody does to us what they did to Dario. It's kill or be killed, Artie, and I'd rather be the one doing the killing."

17

"Mack, I'm going to have to have you stand down."

Bolan couldn't quite believe what Barbara Price, Stony Man's mission controller, had said to him. "Sorry?"

"Stand down. Believe me, the call comes from above my pay grade."

"Who made it, then?"

"You'd have to ask Hal. But I'm guessing above his pay grade, too."

"The President wants me to lay off drug dealers? Since when?"

"I'm just telling you what I've been told, Mack."

"This isn't even a Stony Man op," he argued. "This is personal."

"I know it's not, but we've been providing a great deal of support," Price said.

That much was true. After he left the burning Ivory Wave lab, he had hoofed it back to his motel room. He needed a place to bathe and patch up a few minor wounds, and he still had the key. He wouldn't stay at that motel for another night, but a few more hours couldn't hurt. While he was there, he'd provided Stony Man with the information on the cell phone he had taken from the man who—as his ID had shown, once he was no longer alive to protect his identity—had been named William Carper. He hadn't, incidentally, needed his black

Chevrolet SUV anymore, either, so Bolan had helped himself to that, as well.

But he was up against a brick wall. Carper hadn't financed the lab himself—he had said as much—and though Bolan had destroyed the lab and plenty of product, those with the biggest investment in it could just turn around and start up a new lab, find a new distribution chain. If he couldn't put them out of business, any impact he had made was purely temporary.

After cleaning himself up, he had called in to the Farm to learn what intel the phone might have provided. And instead he got Barbara Price, telling him to back off.

"Tell me what's going on, Barb," he said.

She sighed. "Here's what we found out. Your guy with the phone was a regular caller to a company in Cleveland, called NDC Consolidated Industries."

"Never heard of it."

"It's run by a former Mob figure named Nuncio Chiarello."

"Former?"

"As far as anybody can tell, Mack, everything NDC does is on the up-and-up. Some of it's on the slimy side—they've got financial interests in racetracks and casinos, legal brothels in Nevada, and in Ivory Wave. But they've also got businesses like Laundromats, restaurants, recycling centers, car washes and so on, throughout the Midwest."

"Okay," Bolan said. "We've known all along that everyone thought Ivory Wave was legal, but the tests came back positive for drugs, and I have more evidence of how they've been concocting the stuff. Why does their legit status stop me now, especially when I'm so close to getting who is behind all of it?"

"It's not that. It's—there's something very strange going on in Cleveland. We're just trying to wrap our heads around it, and we're not quite there yet."

Bolan sat on the edge of the bed. Apparently this conversation would take longer than he had expected. "Strange how?"

"Well, as I said, NDC is involved in what appears to be strictly legal businesses. We can't find anybody who has a line on anything crooked about them. Even Nuncio seems to have been clean for years and years. More about that in a minute. What's going on now is that somebody seems to have started a war against him."

"A war?"

"If I didn't know better, Mack," she said, "I'd think it was you. Somebody's been slaughtering people who—if Nuncio was still mobbed up—would be considered soldiers. But now they're colleagues, I guess. Employees. There were eight bodies discovered at a house Nuncio owns. They'd been enjoying a friendly, low-stakes poker game, and somebody came in and shot them up. Another body turned up this morning. This guy worked for an associate of Nuncio's, but not somebody directly on the NDC payroll—a made guy named Artie D'Amato. Artie isn't on the straight-and-narrow like Nuncio, and neither is his boss, Dominic Chiarello, Nuncio's brother. Dominic just finished a twenty-five-year stint as a guest of the state of Ohio and went home to Cleveland. Almost immediately the bodies started piling up."

"But one of the bodies is his own guy?"

"Loyalties there are, let's say, fungible," Price explained. "While Dominic was away, Artie maintained an arm's-length relationship with Nuncio. They didn't do any direct business together that we can determine, since Nuncio was straight and Artie wasn't. But the relationship might have been a complicated one that could have involved some sort of exchange of funds, in either or both directions. For sure, Artie was helping to support Dominic's wife. I haven't been able to pin down exactly what the link between Artie and Nuncio was, but it's possible that an attack on one of his guys could be considered an attack on Nuncio. Or it could be retaliation by Nuncio. It's hard to say at this point."

"So somebody you can't name, but who could be the President, wants me to stay out of the fight?"

"There are all sorts of interested parties here. Earlier I said that Nuncio appears to be clean. That's the appearance, but we don't know if it's a fact. The FBI has somebody under deep cover who has climbed fairly high up in the organization. They don't want a freelancer coming in and possibly disrupting an investigation they've put years and a lot of money into."

"And that's what I am? A freelancer?"

"You know what I mean. People at the Bureau don't know you exist, Mack."

"Just what is it they're investigating?" Bolan asked. "You said the record was Nuncio has been clean for years."

"But not forever, and before you started this crusade there were others who were suspicious of Ivory Wave. Nuncio and Dominic Chiarello left a lot of bodies in their wake as they were coming up. They finally busted Dominic on racketeering charges and sent him away, but the Bureau would still like to pin some murders on both brothers."

"And there's no statute of limitations on those," Bolan said.

"Speaking of murder, there's another thing," she added. "There have been a lot of hitters going into Cleveland over the past twenty-four hours. Guys from Chicago, New York, Miami, Vegas and so on. It's like somebody's throwing a killers convention."

"Or like somebody who's been out of the game for a while is expecting a war."

"You could see it that way."

Bolan saw it exactly that way. "So I'm just supposed to let this Ivory Wave thing go, because the FBI is worried a 'freelancer' might get in the way of an investigation of somebody who is, according to all appearances, not doing anything illegal."

"That's the word I've been asked to pass along. I'm passing it."

"Okay," Bolan said. "You told me."

"Should I even ask what you're going to do?" Price asked.

"Do you really need to?"

She laughed, but seemed to quickly remember that she shouldn't. "Mack…"

"Will it help if I just don't tell you what I'm doing?"

"It couldn't hurt."

"Well, if you don't ask, I won't say."

"Deal," she said. "Be safe, Mack."

"Always." He ended the call and snatched up his zippered ordnance bag. He winced. Maybe not always totally safe, he thought—the night's activities had taken a toll on him. A person didn't drive a truck through a building without suffering some aches and pains down the line.

He was fresh out of trucks. But he was already in Cleveland, home of NDC Consolidated Industries. No way he was leaving without paying a visit.

Still, walking into a war was usually not a good idea. Not that he hadn't done it before, but he liked to know what he was getting into when he did.

He thought for a moment, then dialed another phone number.

Bolan had carried out his own one-man war against the Mafia, and he had made a lot of enemies in the organized crime community. Few accomplishments in life made him more proud.

But his immersion in that world had taught him a lesson that shouldn't have been surprising, on the face of it, but was just the same. As in every other community of human beings, not everyone was as bad as its worst members.

As an example, there was Sheldon Wylie.

Sheldon Wylie was no more Sicilian than Bolan himself. He had entered that world as a boy, not through an accident of birth but of death—that of his parents, in a house fire that he alone survived. With no living grandparents or other family to take him in, he had gone to an orphanage, then entered the foster-care system. After a couple of wretched experiences, he had been taken in by his next-door neighbor, Rosa D'Errico, the near-saintly wife of a thug and murderer named Betto D'Errico.

Wylie had been adopted by the D'Erricos and raised as one of their own, along with their other three sons. All the boys had gone on to become powerful figures in the organized crime community, including Sheldon Wylie. But Wylie's heart had never been in it. He had felt he'd had no choice. His adoptive parents hadn't offered to pay for college, and by the time he reached adulthood, he had no other role models to help him find another path.

When Bolan went up against Vinny D'Errico, the most bloodthirsty of the brothers, he'd found himself outnumbered, outgunned and in trouble. He had encountered Sheldon Wylie, had seen something decent in the man, and Wylie had, for his part, found something about Bolan that he trusted. More than that, he'd found an example. He helped Bolan, Bolan helped him, and together they defeated Vinny D'Errico and dismantled his operation.

Since then, Wylie had kept a hand in the Family business, but only in a very limited fashion. And he had contacted Bolan from time to time, telling him about particularly heinous crimes he'd heard about. Bolan had acted on his intel and always found him trustworthy.

So it was Sheldon Wylie's number he called from his motel room in Cleveland.

The man answered with a hesitant "Hello?"

"Wylie," Bolan said. "It's me."

"It's...oh. Hi. What's up?"

"I need something."

"I figured you did. You don't normally call me. But considering the number of times I've called you, well...just name it."

"I need an introduction."

"Who to?"

"Anybody in Cleveland, pretty much."

"In Cleveland, in the Family business?"

"Right."

"I know a couple of people," Wylie said.

"Ever heard of Nuncio Chiarello?"

"I don't think so, no."

"How about Dominic Chiarello?"

"Yes. I don't know him. But I know people who know people who do."

"Can you make some calls? Without putting yourself in harm's way?" Bolan asked.

"Of course."

"I'd appreciate that," Bolan said. "Here's the name I'll be using...."

18

Once the arrangements had been made, Bolan drove to the Cleveland Hopkins International Airport. He parked in short-term parking, left the ticket in the SUV and hiked through the lines of cars to the nearby Holiday Inn Express. He checked in under a false identity that wasn't the Tom Kenner name he had asked that Wylie use or the Matt Cooper alias he had used in Makin. In the privacy of his room he went online and learned the location of the NDC Consolidated Industries building in downtown Cleveland. He retrieved the vehicle from the lot, drove into the city, parked a few blocks away, then walked over, making a circuit of the entire block. It was an area in transition, industrial turning slowly into business, or the other way around. The building hadn't been there long, Bolan guessed, and he suspected Nuncio had done some serious remodeling, as well.

There was a restaurant on the next block, a diner that served sandwiches and burgers, with windows facing toward the corner. Bolan went in and ordered a meal. He sat at a window table and watched the NDC building for most of an hour.

There wasn't much to see. The structure was gray stone and anonymous, except for a name plaque by the front door that identified the building's occupant. It was six stories tall, with a few windows, mostly on the side that faced toward the lake, though if there were lake views, it was only from the upper floor. There was an underground parking garage. Only one car went in while Bolan watched, a black Lincoln. When the steel gate slid back to admit it, Bolan caught a glimpse of a couple of guys in dark clothes on the inside, checking the car's occupants as it entered.

The building's front entrance was on Rockwell Avenue. The door was clad in brass, and Bolan figured that was probably steel under that. A couple of people came and went, including a guy who parked right in front, then fetched a stack of about a dozen pizzas from the back of his truck. Every time the door opened, Bolan saw more guys on the inside. No one ever opened the door alone.

What he saw looked like a building under siege, or getting ready for one. What he didn't see was an easy way inside.

That didn't bother him too much. He wasn't used to taking the easy way.

Having seen what he could, he returned to the hotel, parking this time in the long-term lot. He wasn't expected until morning, so he returned to the hotel. He watched a movie, which was a rare luxury, worked out in the gym, enjoyed a leisurely dinner, then went to sleep early and got in a good nine hours. In the morning he had breakfast, then walked over to the airport.

A few minutes after the first flight arrived from Las Vegas, he went outside and caught a cab. He gave the driver the address he had been given. The cab driver stopped in front of a coffee shop on a business block not too far from downtown.

"Here you go," the man said. Bolan paid him, giving a tip that was neither stingy nor generous, and got out of the car.

A Closed sign hung in the coffee shop's door, and the interior lights were off. Bolan stood in front of the place for a few moments, uncertain of his next step. But then he saw movement inside the darkened shop, and the door opened.

A huge man filled the doorway, and he caught Bolan's eye. "Kenner?" he asked.

"That's right."

"I'm Massimo Chiarello. Come on inside."

Bolan gave Massimo the same once-over the other man gave him. The guy was huge, taller than Bolan, and with sixty or seventy pounds on him. He wore a gold tracksuit and plenty of gold jewelry: chains around his neck, a wristwatch on one arm and a bracelet on the other, rings. His knuckles were recently skinned and there was scar tissue around his eyes and nose. He put out his hand and Bolan shook it, both men squeezing tighter than was necessary but quitting before it got obnoxious.

Inside the coffee shop, another man sat at a table in the back, watching the doorway. An H&K submachine gun sat on the table in front of him. "Massimo's gonna pat you down," the other man said.

"Sure." Bolan had expected as much. He was wearing a dark blue ribbed T-shirt, jeans and a navy blue blazer that hid his shoulder holster. The Beretta 93-R was tucked under his arm, and he'd known coming in that he would have to give it up. He also knew that when he did, he would be unarmed, in the middle of a den of vipers. There was no way around it, though. He opened the blazer, revealing the piece. Massimo lifted it out with two fingers, put it on a nearby table and continued the search.

"No problem getting that here on the plane?" Massimo asked.

"Not if you know the right people."

"Tell me who they are, so maybe I won't lose my fucking luggage so often," Massimo said with a grin.

Massimo gave him a thorough frisking. Bolan had been right not to try to sneak in another gun or even a knife. When they were done, Massimo gave the Beretta to the guy sitting down and nodded toward a doorway at the back of the shop. "Back here."

Bolan followed him through the doorway, which took them into a narrow hall that led past a small kitchen. Through a second door, they entered a large room with a few tables and a couple dozen chairs. There was a big urn-style coffeemaker on one table, and the room smelled like old coffee and cigarette smoke. More bruisers sat around one of the tables, and an older guy, gray haired but hard-looking, sat by himself. He rose when Bolan came in.

"Artie, this is Kenner," Massimo stated.

"Thanks for coming," Artie said.

"Heard you could use some guys," Bolan said. He assumed the man was Artie D'Amato, but knew better than to ask.

Artie indicated one of the chairs at his table. "Sit."

Bolan sat.

"You come well recommended," Artie said. "How come I never heard of you?"

"Because I'm good at what I do," Bolan told him. "Means I don't make a lot of noise. I get in, get the job done and get gone."

"That's a good quality."

"I think so."

He felt Artie's gaze, appraising him. "He carrying?" he asked Massimo.

"He had a Beretta."

"Good Italian piece. But you're not Italian," Artie said. "Or Sicilian."

"I didn't realize there was a national origin qualification."

"There's not. It's just easier sometimes."

Bolan started to get out of the chair. "If you don't want me—"

Artie waved him back down. "No, sit, sit. Nobody's saying that."

"Okay, then."

"How do we know you're as good as you say?" Artie asked.

Bolan looked around the room. Six men in all, every one of them looking dangerous. "Any of them you can do without?"

"That's it?" Artie asked. "You'd just kill one of these guys on my say-so?"

"That's what the job is, right?"

Artie chuckled. "That's part of it. Here's what's going on. There's kind of a conflict brewing, between my man Dominic and his brother. Family history can be tough, right?"

"My parents died when I was a kid," Bolan said. "So I don't know."

"Take my word for it. Anyway, there's already been some trouble, and we think there'll be more. Dom has been away for a long time, and I was more or less associated with Nuncio until he came back. But now that he's back, things have taken a turn for the worse. We're hiring some guys to help out while we build Dom's organization back up. Looks like Nuncio might try to interfere. Your job would be to protect Dom and his interests, and to take the fight straight to Nuncio if need be. You okay with that?"

"I can do without the details," Bolan said. "Point me in the right direction and turn me loose."

"There could be a lot of waiting around before there's any action."

"But you pay either way, right?" Bolan asked.

"We pay either way." Artie named a number.

"Okay, then."

"You're in?"

"Isn't that what okay means? I've never spent time in Cleveland, but I thought you spoke English here."

Artie laughed again. "Give him his piece back," he said. "I think Kenner is gonna work out just fine."

ARTIE D'AMATO HAD been correct about one thing: there was
a lot of waiting around. Bolan didn't ask a lot of questions
or volunteer much, but he listened and watched. He learned
that Dominic Chiarello had brought in eleven men, including
him, from out of town, to add to the fourteen that Dominic
and Artie had between them. And he learned that, although
Massimo was Nuncio's son, he had sided with Dominic. Nobody knew if Nuncio had discovered that yet, but it was expected that when he did, the waiting would end and the war
would be on.

When it did come, Bolan hoped the men around him would
be ready. They were all hard cases. A couple were ex-mil-
itary—Bolan recognized it in their posture, the easy way
they carried themselves, comfortable in their own skins. One
looked like a JSOC veteran, and he had a tattoo that Bolan
had seen on some Navy SEALs. He and Bolan didn't have
to speak to share a mutual respect based on the understanding that both were battle-tested warriors. But sitting around
drinking coffee and eating pastries wasn't preparing them
for combat. Artie provided everybody with H&K MP5s and
boxes of 9 mm Parabellum rounds. Most guys had 32-round
magazines, but a handful got 100-round drum magazines.
They weren't allowed to fire them in the space behind the coffee shop, though, and except for a few guys who went out to
Dominic's house, that's where they stayed. There were other
rooms back there, some stocked with mattresses, and there
was a bathroom with a shower stall. Bolan thought about the
nice hotel room he was paying for, by the airport.

But staying there wouldn't put him close to Nuncio, and
the more he heard, the more he understood that it was Nuncio, not Dominic, who was behind the Ivory Wave epidemic.

So he waited, along with the rest.

19

"Sitting around here is driving me fuckin' nuts," Massimo said. "I've gotta get some air. You want to come?"

Nico shook his head. "I'll stay put," he said. "You go if you want. I'll cover for you."

"Thanks," Massimo said. He had wanted Nico to come along. Since he had finished off Dario, he hadn't had a chance to be alone with Nico anyplace that it was safe to kill the guy.

Nico was loyal to Dominic, but loyalty went only so far. Anybody could be bought for the right price, and Massimo didn't know what Nico's price would be. He didn't want to find out by learning that Nico had told Nuncio that it had been Massimo who had shot up his poker game. Things would come to a head between his father and his uncle soon enough, and then it would all be out in the open.

Until then, he didn't want to burn any bridges. He needed his options left open, just in case.

Still, he had to do something to burn off nervous energy. Not just anything—he knew what he wanted to do. The only thing he had thought about for more than fifteen seconds at a time these past several days.

He had to kill.

The power he felt when someone's life passed from them, at his hands, was intoxicating. Addicting. He couldn't get enough.

He took a walk around the neighborhood. The daylight was fading fast; lights were already on around the block, and a couple of stars had just appeared in the sky. He walked faster, out of the immediate neighborhood and into streets where he wouldn't be recognized.

The blocks shifted from mostly businesses to largely residential. There were a couple of shops with apartments upstairs over them, and then the shops were gone and the homes separated by patches of grass, driveways and garages. Massimo kept walking, his fists stuffed into his pockets. Finally he saw a young couple pull their Toyota into a driveway ahead of him. Both were white, maybe early thirties, fit and healthy-looking. They got cloth bags containing groceries from the back of the car and carried them into the house. Massimo looked quickly up and down the block, didn't see anybody watching. He followed the couple inside, through the door they had closed but not locked.

When he entered, he shut the door softly, then threw the dead bolt. It clicked, and the couple broke off a cheerful conversation in the kitchen. "Hello?" the man asked. "Bill, is that—"

He came into the kitchen doorway and stopped, a jar of organic peanut butter in his hands. "I'm not Bill," Massimo said.

"I can see that. What do you want?"

"Nothing you're prepared to give."

"Sherry, call 911," the guy said. "Look, you—"

"No phone calls," Massimo said. He started toward the man.

The guy threw the peanut butter jar like a fastball. Massimo swatted it away, but it hurt his hand. "Sherry, run!" the guy shouted as he charged Massimo.

He caught Massimo, grappled with him. The woman came out of the kitchen, trying to go past the men to the front door. Massimo wrenched his right arm free of the man's grip, threw a quick, powerful jab into his solar plexus and the man doubled around Massimo's fist. The woman gave a scream of terror as she tried to pass, but Massimo kicked her in the side of the knee. He heard a cracking sound and she screamed again, in pain this time, as she fell.

The man swore and put his hands on Massimo's throat. He had strong arms, which Massimo credited to tennis, maybe. Or swimming—he had that kind of build. Tears filled the man's eyes and he was snarling, spittle flecking his lips. Massimo stood there for a moment, letting the man choke him, letting the certainty that the man would soon die fill his spirit, and then he broke the man's grip with ease, cocked his fist back and drove it with all the muscle he could put behind it into the man's nose. It pulped, cartilage tearing, blood fountaining from it. Massimo hit him again, in the left eye this time. The man went to his knees, wordless sounds issuing from his mouth along with mixed blood and saliva. Massimo hit him once more, putting the man flat on the floor.

Meanwhile, his wife was still screaming, trying to drag herself to the door with her useless leg trailing behind her. Massimo went to her, put a gentle hand on her shoulder. "Does it hurt?" he asked softly.

"Yes! Yes, it hurts!"

"I'll make it stop."

Without another word, Massimo wrapped his hand around her face, grabbed her by the cheek and twisted her head toward him with a sudden jerk. He could hear her neck bones snap, and she went limp in his hands.

The man was still trying to move, writhing on the floor. The pain had to be incredible, Massimo knew, but even that was probably secondary to his rage and terror. Whether he knew what Massimo had done, or only guessed, Massimo couldn't tell.

He went back to the man and picked up his right hand off

the floor. The man tried to jerk it away, but his strength was ebbing fast. When he started to scream, Massimo ripped off part of his shirt and jammed it deep into the man's mouth. Then he began breaking bones, a few at a time. When the man finally lost consciousness, the entertainment value dissipated, so Massimo finished him off quickly.

As he left the house, he found himself hoping that his father would take action against Uncle Dom soon. He had just killed two people, but he wanted more, and he wanted it now.

"WHERE'S YOUR BROTHER?" Nuncio asked. "He's never around anymore."

"I don't know, Papa," Gino said.

"Well, why the hell not? Don't you talk to him?"

"More sometimes than others," Gino replied. "Lately, not so much."

Nuncio caught Cosimo's eye, then Brendan's. "Brothers. Family. When did it all get so complicated?"

"Family has always been complicated," Cosimo said.

"Not like this."

"I'm not so sure about that," Brendan said. "The Civil War, brother against brother, remember? And didn't Dickens write something about unhappy families?"

"Maybe he did," Nuncio said. "But I'm not talking about other families, I'm talking about this one. What the hell has happened to us? Gino and Massimo not talking. It'd break their mother's heart, God rest her soul. And that brother of mine, away for all those years and then he gets back and can't even spare me a kind word or a few minutes of his time. I don't understand. I don't understand this world we're living in."

They were in Nuncio's office on the top floor of the building on Rockwell. It was luxuriously appointed, with leather furniture and a floor of fine Italian marble, covered in part by expensive antique Persian rugs. His desktop held a humidor filled with pricey Cuban cigars, the one vice he still allowed himself that broke the law. Nuncio had done well for himself, and he liked to be surrounded by fine things. His house was the same way, though he had not taken as much pleasure in that once his wife was gone.

But he hadn't been home in more than twenty-four hours, and wasn't sure when he would be again. He and his guys were all holed up in the office building where they could keep an eye on one another and defend against what he was increasingly sure were attacks on his interests coordinated by Dominic. None of it had started until Dom came out of the joint. Since he'd been back, it had been nonstop.

Dom would either come for him here, or he would take it to Dom. Which way it went didn't matter to Nuncio, as long as there would be a reckoning.

He picked up his phone off the desk and punched Massimo's number. On the other end, it rang four times, then Massimo's voice came on. "Leave me a message," it said.

"This is your father. Where the hell you been? Call me!" He ended the call and dropped the phone again. He crossed to the window, looked out toward the lake, then down at the street. Traffic passed by, people who carried on with their business, blissfully unaware that a man's family was falling apart and his life might be in danger.

Cosimo cleared his throat. Nuncio whirled on him. "What?" he snapped, his fists clenched.

"Nunce, you've got to accept the possibility."

"What possibility? What are you talking about?"

"That he's gone over. To Dom's side."

"Massimo is my son!"

"So's Gino," Cosimo pointed out. "And Gino's sitting right here. Massimo's not, so what does that tell you? He could be moving against you. All the files from the safe at the plant were stolen, all the formulas. They may be starting their own operation. What does all of that tell you?"

"That I should have worn a rubber that time. Is that what you want me to say?" He sat down heavily in his desk chair, put his elbows on the mahogany surface and buried his face in his hands. "My son and my brother both betraying me, together? It's too much. It's just too fucking much!"

"Papa," Gino said, his voice pleading, "you don't know that yet."

"Neither one will answer my goddamn phone calls. My world is falling apart and neither one of them is here. Marco's right."

"I'm just saying," Cosimo said. "You've got to accept that it's a possibility, so you can take appropriate action if you find out it's true."

Brendan was sitting on a leather couch, his arms folded over his chest, looking vaguely uncomfortable. "What do you think, Brendan?"

"I don't know you as well as Marco does," the young man replied.

"You've been with us for what, a couple years now, right?"

"Nearly."

"So, long enough to form impressions."

"You're putting me on the spot, Nunce."

"Damn right." He kept his gaze leveled on the young man. "You've worked with Massimo plenty. You know him."

"He's a hard one to figure out," Brendan said. "He keeps his own counsel, I guess you'd say. But yeah, he definitely looks up to Dominic. *Worships* might be too strong a word, but not by a lot."

"So my own flesh and blood—the brother I shared a womb with, and the son who's the fruit of my loins—want to kill me."

"You don't know that yet, Nunce," Cosimo said.

Nuncio slapped his chest. "I know it here, Marco. I know it here. They've turned against me, and they want to see me dead."

"Maybe."

"Definitely. What's worse is they think that knowledge alone will break me. Make me weak."

"But it won't, will it?" Gino asked.

"Hell no," Nuncio said. "The only thing it'll do is make me more determined. They think they can betray me? I'll spit on their graves."

"You're getting yourself worked up, Nunce," Cosimo said.

"*They're* getting me worked up. I didn't start any of this."

"Papa, maybe it's not what you think," Gino said. "Maybe—"

"Maybe nothing!" Nuncio exploded. "I know he's your brother, Gino, but he's in league with the devil now."

"The devil?" Brendan asked.

Nuncio looked at the young man, unsure of how much he really knew. Then he looked away, picked up a gold lighter set into a block of heavy stone that had once been part of the Berlin Wall. He flicked the lighter and stared into the flame. "Growing up, we did some things, Dom and I. We were hell-raisers, you might say. It was a different era, and we went along with whatever had to be done. We took what our father had started and made it into something bigger, something better. But Cleveland was a tough city in those days, and we had to be tougher. I won't say I'm proud of everything we did, but I'm proud that we did them, if you get my meaning. Proud we had what it took.

"But Dom, he was more than proud. He enjoyed the life— not just the women and the cars and the good booze and the fancy clothes. He liked the hurting and the killing. Some men are just that way, I guess. And I think maybe Massimo, he's like that, too. I wasn't—I mean, I did it, but not just for the doing.

"So what I think now is, I think that Dom believes I'm soft. He believes that because he liked doing those things and I didn't, that means he can and I can't. That now he's out, he can just move in on all I've built while he's been away. He can take it from me, take it over, because he's the strong one and I'm the weak one."

"But you're not weak, Papa!" Gino insisted.

Sometimes, Nuncio thought, that young man was pathetic. If he'd had half of Massimo's steel in him… He pushed the thought from his head.

"You're right, son," he said. "I'm not weak. But Dominic won't believe that unless he's shown. That's why I'm going to demonstrate to him that he's not the only strong one here."

"Demonstrate?" Cosimo asked. "How?"

Nuncio put the big lighter down with a heavy thump. "Brendan, bring a couple of those out-of-towners in here. You know the ones I mean."

"I think so, Nunce."

"The kind who can make a statement," Nuncio said. "It's time to get this party started."

20

Bolan watched Massimo come back into the big, open room behind the coffee shop. He walked with his shoulders back, his head cocked at a slight angle. He looked as if he had just swallowed a smile and if he relented for an instant, it would pop back out. His cheeks were flushed, and as he passed Bolan caught a whiff of fresh, ripe sweat.

And there was blood on his clothing that hadn't been there before.

Maybe he had cut himself shaving. Maybe he'd helped someone who'd been hit by a bus, or had been in a fight and bloodied somebody's nose.

Bolan didn't think so, though.

He had seen plenty of violent men over the years. He knew a little something about them, especially the worst of them, the ones who didn't use violence as simply a tool to achieve a desired result, but who enjoyed it for its own sake. They had a way of carrying themselves, a way they walked and a way they looked, that could tell the close observer that they weren't to be trifled with. They set themselves above the rest of humanity. There were two classes of people—them and those who could be their victims.

Massimo, he thought, had bought into that.

He would fight and he would kill, just because he took pleasure in dispensing suffering to others, and even more pleasure in dealing out that final end. He liked to hear their breathing stop, liked to see the light vanish from their eyes.

He watched Massimo cross the room, pour some coffee into a foam cup and taste it. He made a face. Bolan didn't blame him for that—a whole coffee shop was out there, and they were drinking bitter brew from an industrial-size pot. But Massimo downed the coffee as he stood there, then crushed the cup in his hand. Droplets of hot coffee got on his skin, and bits of white debris from the cup snowed toward the floor. Massimo ignored all that and threw the cup at the steel wastebasket by the table. It hit the rim and bounced off. Massimo didn't notice.

He took a seat off by himself. Some of the other men looked his way, but no one approached. Everyone knew he was the son of their target, and some of them had confessed to Bolan that they weren't entirely sure where his loyalties might lie.

Bolan was sure now. He had seen it in every move Massimo had made since he'd walked in that door. His father had prevented Massimo from killing—he was going straight, after all, running legit businesses, and he had wanted Massimo to join him in that endeavor. So Massimo had grown up hearing stories about his father's crimes, his murders, and knew that his uncle was in prison for his crimes. Probably he had looked up to Dominic, who reportedly had never ratted out his fellow mobsters, even when it might have shortened his own sentence.

Nuncio had stunted Massimo's growth into the criminal, the killer he had always wanted to be. Bigger than the other boys and the other men, Massimo had wanted to revel in his sheer physicality, wanted people to be afraid of him. But they hadn't been, because he had been Nuncio's kid, and therefore walked the straight and narrow.

Dominic had come home from prison and let the young man off his leash.

Bolan had no doubts about Massimo's loyalty. He would kill for Dominic Chiarello, would perhaps even die for him, if necessary. And he would kill his own father with his bare hands, just because he could.

Just because his uncle had given him permission.

ARTIE D'AMATO CAME into the big room and stopped in the doorway. He called out four names, including Tom Kenner's. "Let's go," he said.

"Where to?" someone asked.

"Dom's place," Artie said. "We're moving him and Annamaria over here, where they'll be safer."

"We got a place to put them?" That was a guy named Micelli, one of the out-of-town shooters.

"There are a couple of rooms upstairs," Massimo answered. "They'll be comfortable there."

Bolan went along with them, as requested. He didn't have any reason to argue, and he figured some up-close-and-personal time with Dominic Chiarello couldn't hurt. He still hadn't learned who at NDC was responsible for the decision to go into the Ivory Wave business, though he was leaning toward Nuncio, since from the sound of it, although the company name included his initial, Dominic hadn't been involved in business decisions while he was in prison.

Artie loaded them into a black Lincoln Navigator and drove them out of town. About thirty minutes later they had entered a neighborhood of elegant homes set far apart, with lush landscaping and manicured lawns. Artie slowed the SUV before a wrought-iron gate with three men standing behind it. He rolled down his window and spoke a couple of words to the men, and they activated the gate. It parted in the middle and the two halves swung wide. Artie thumbed his window up as he drove the Navigator up the drive. The house at the end of the drive had the look of a French château from the Renaissance era, except scaled down and updated.

"Nice place," said a guy named Bennie. He was from Chicago. Bolan had claimed to be from Vegas, and he worried a little that someone else from there would press him about people he knew. He had a basic knowledge of some of the players in Nevada, but it wouldn't stand up under an intense interrogation. So far, he had been able to establish himself as a quiet guy, and the other men hadn't tried to engage him in any extended conversations.

"Dom's always been a good earner," Artie said. "Smart guy, made some good investments early on." He braked the Lincoln to a halt in front of the doorway. Three similar dark SUVs were already parked there. From the drive, four steps led up to a wooden door that two pro basketball players could pass through, one sitting on the other's shoulders. Two bruisers flanked the door, H&K MP5s in their hands.

"Get out," Artie said. "But don't go inside the house unless I tell you to."

The men did as they were told. They nodded to the men on the steps, but no words passed between them. Bolan had been in similar situations countless times. Men were brought together from different states, different countries. They had different political beliefs, came from different races and economic backgrounds. The only thing they had in common was that they were all trained to kill, and ready to do so when they were ordered. For that reason, they shared a comradeship that often went unspoken. When you knew the guy beside you might be dead any minute, or you might be dead unless he did his job, words often seemed beside the point, and inadequate at best.

Artie went inside and the door closed behind him. Bolan eyed the shadowed parts of the lawn, where tall trees and

thick shrubbery might provide cover for the enemy. A few
minutes passed, and the door opened again. This time an older
man who had to be Dominic Chiarello came out behind Artie.
Artie carried a suitcase, and so did the guy behind Dominic, one of the hired shooters. Behind him came a slender
woman who could only be Annamaria. She was in her late
fifties probably, but well kept, with some plastic surgery to
keep her flesh tight. Her hair was artificially blond, her jaw
taut. Some wrinkles on her neck gave away her age, but for
the most part she made Chiarello look like a cradle robber.

Chiarello himself was completely gray, and he looked older
than he probably was, which Bolan attributed to his time
in prison. His face was heavily lined, his eyes hooded. He
looked strong, but Bolan guessed that now that he was on
the outside, with more on his mind, that wouldn't last long.
He wore a dark blazer over a silk shirt and linen pants, and
the jacket's structure couldn't disguise the way his shoulders
slanted away from his muscular neck. His waist was trim,
his chest deep. He glanced over the men gathered around the
doorway, acknowledging them with a couple of slight nods.
Annamaria didn't even look at them. Bolan wondered if she
was somehow ashamed of needing their protection. Maybe
what shamed her was the fact that everybody knew how the
beautiful home and the cosmetic surgery and the expensive
leather suitcases had been paid for. She'd had plenty of time
to get used to it, but she had also been able to spend much
of the past twenty-five years pretending it wasn't true. Now
it had all been brought back in a very real, undeniable way.

Artie walked quickly between the groups of men, laying
out the plan. Most of those stationed at the house would be
joining them. Four men would ride in the lead vehicle, three
in the second with Chiarello, three in the third with Annamaria and the rest bringing up the rear. Once they reached
the building that housed the coffee shop, they would drive

around to the alley running behind it and unload by the back door. All the men would get out then, and congregate around Dominic's car. Once he was inside they would form the same barrier around Annamaria. Inside the building, they would have an upstairs room in the building's center, with no windows. It would take a wrecking ball, or an RPG attack, to get to them in there.

They split up and entered their assigned vehicles. The driver of the lead one rolled slowly to the gate, where the men standing guard let them out, but as soon as he was on the street, he hit the gas. The other drivers followed suit, and in moments all four SUVs were tearing down the quiet residential street. Bolan, in the front seat of the second car with Chiarello directly behind him, was reminded of convoys in Iraq, where contractors and soldiers alike ignored every traffic law in favor of reaching their destinations quickly and alive.

What he didn't like was how close the vehicles were staying to one another. This wasn't Iraq, after all—there was no other traffic, no danger that some other vehicle, possibly one loaded with explosives, would weave in between the convoy vehicles. But, as in Iraq, a roadside bomb could take out multiple vehicles if they were too bunched up.

He was about to say something to the driver, to encourage him to drop back a few car lengths, when the machine guns opened up.

21

They had just entered the first turn of an S-curve that cut between a small neighborhood park on one side and a high school on the other. Both stretches of roadway were dark, until muzzle flashes tore the night at the same instant that window glass shattered and there was a noise like a rainfall of pebbles hitting the sides of the vehicle. The driver let out a grunt of pain, but Bolan wasn't sure if he'd been hit by a round or by windshield glass.

The front car was hit by at least a few rounds, and the driver's response was to push the accelerator to the floor. The driver next to Bolan was starting to do the same thing. Bolan grabbed his arm. "Stop the car," he said.

"But—"

Bolan already knew the arguments the man would make, and they didn't have time to go through them. "Just stop," he said. "Block the road if you can." He didn't want the SUV carrying Annamaria to go past, either. To emphasize his point, he gave the wheel a tug toward him and turned the key, killing the engine.

His commanding tone did the trick, and the vehicle fishtailed as it jerked to a shuddering stop, tail toward the curb. The position put Chiarello in the safest position, hard to get to by the gunmen slightly ahead of the SUV on right and left. Bolan was out the door before it even came to a full stop, dropping to his stomach on the asphalt, his H&K aimed at where he had seen the last muzzle blast from the park. As soon as he saw another one, he squeezed the trigger and sent a dozen rounds sailing through the dark. Hot brass shell casings clinked to the street around him. The shooter cried out, and the flame from his gun barrel tilted toward the sky.

Answering fire still came from the other side of the street, though, somewhere near the school building. Bolan suspected the shooter on that side was using the building itself for cover. He gained his feet and ran in a crouch to the corner of the big SUV, then sighted on the near corner of the school. It had occurred to him that there were only two shooters here, which was why he had wanted the vehicles to stop before getting deeper into the S-curve.

He saw the second gunman in light reflecting off a window of the school building, before the man had even settled on his next target. Bolan squeezed off another long burst, and the man fell.

Bolan returned to the SUV and stuck his head in the door. "You okay, Mr. Chiarello?" he asked.

"Yeah," Chiarello said. "You got those bastards."

"That's right," Bolan replied. "But they're only the beginning."

"What do you mean?" the driver asked.

"Two guys? Nobody would send two guys on an ambush like this," Bolan explained. "They were just to get us distracted, not paying attention on the next couple of curves. We'd speed up, then we'd slow down for the tightest curve, thinking we were in the clear. That's when the bigger force would hit us."

"We should turn around," the driver said. He reached for the key.

"Mr. Chiarello," Bolan said quickly, "if we do that, you might get out of this alive. But you'll only have taken out two of their men. And, honestly, you'll look like a coward if you run from this. We have one chance to make a real statement here, but you'll have to trust me for a few minutes."

In the dim light he could see Chiarello considering. He didn't take long to make up his mind, which Bolan appreciated. "I don't know who you are, but if I had ten more guys with your balls I could rule the entire Midwest," he said. "Do what you've got to do."

"It'll mean leaving you here with limited protection. And your wife, too. For a little while."

"Whatever it takes," Chiarello said.

Bolan didn't delay. He put Chiarello and his wife into the third SUV, and had them duck down behind the seats. He put two shooters in the front, including the one who had been wounded most severely, bleeding from the clavicle, and took the rest with him. As they cut across the schoolyard, he explained what would have to pass for a plan.

They had nine men. He didn't know how many would be waiting around the bend, or how closely they'd be bunched. But they would be watching the road, starting to think that their targets weren't coming after all. They had let the first vehicle go by, guessing—correctly—that Chiarello wouldn't be in the lead car. But by now they'd be worried that maybe that one would turn around and come back. They would be on edge, having heard the exchange of gunfire and not knowing what the results had been.

All those factors would work in favor of Bolan and his crew. As would the fact that they'd be coming from behind the gunmen, instead of from the road. If there were other shooters on the far side of the road, they would be safe behind whatever cover they had taken. And if they were all on the far side, then Bolan's plan would be a disaster because he and his men would have to cross the street on foot. They'd be sliced to ribbons.

Bolan had to admit that he was impressed by the quality of the men hired on Chiarello's behalf. They had never trained together, never had to fight as a unit, but they moved through the dark with speed and silence, their weapons at the ready. In less than two minutes they had crossed the school grounds and passed through somebody's side yard.

Ahead of them were the men from the other team. Bolan counted seven. They were huddled together behind a thick hedge, probably discussing their options. He couldn't tell if there were more across the street, but he'd find out soon enough.

For now, the task ahead couldn't be easier. The way they were grouped meant he could put them all down himself. With nine guns, they would never stand a chance. It was almost unsportsmanlike.

Then again, Bolan wasn't here for sport.

He gave the signal, and he and his guys fired short bursts, cutting the men down where they stood. From the far side of the street, somebody opened fire at them, but it was only two guys, and they didn't last long.

When they were finished, Bolan led his team back across the schoolyard. The sound of distant sirens cut the quiet night. They had to move out in a hurry, now that the path was clear, or there would be a lot of difficult questions directed their way.

They reached the cars and split up, returning to their designated spots, except Bolan got into the third car with Dominic and Annamaria Chiarello and sent two men up to what had become the lead car. They were barely out of the S-curve when they met the first SUV, which had eventually doubled back for them. It let them pass, then made a screaming U-turn and followed.

They didn't stop again until they were in the alley behind the coffee shop. There, the men did as they'd been told, forming a human shield for the Chiarellos. When the couple was safely inside, the men filtered in, going back to the common room. Only there did the tension finally break. Pouring coffee and making sandwiches and lighting smokes, the men started talking loudly, telling those who had stayed behind what had happened, cracking jokes. Bolan recognized the syndrome. During the action they had held it all in, keeping themselves together. Once they were on safe ground, they had to let the tension out. Some men did it by fighting, some through sex. Here, those weren't very viable options.

While a doctor tended to the wounded, Artie came for Bolan. "Kenner," he said, his mouth a thin, straight line, "come with me."

Bolan rose from his chair, downed the dregs of his coffee and flipped the empty cup into a wastebasket. He felt several pairs of eyes burning into him as he was led from the room.

"MR. KENNER," DOMINIC CHIARELLO said. He took Bolan's hand and gave it a firm shake. "I didn't have a chance to thank you earlier."

"No need," Bolan said. "I was hired to fight for your side. Long as I get paid, I'm happy."

They were in a kind of sitting room that had been set up for the Chiarellos. The upper floors had been apartments once, and though this one was no longer furnished like one, it did the job. This room had a couple of chairs and a couch, thrift-store modern, but serviceable. Bolan saw a closed door at the back of the room, and he figured there was a bedroom behind it. Annamaria was probably in there. To get in, he and Artie had passed a small kitchen, and a glance through another open door had revealed a toilet and sink. "Still. Once I heard everything that you did, I was glad we had you with us. You really took charge."

"It's just who I am, I guess."

"Well, Mrs. Chiarello and I are grateful to you. That could have gone a lot worse."

"It could have," Bolan agreed.

"How much do you know about what we're doing here?"

"Only what Artie told me. And Massimo. There's trouble between you and your brother. You've been expecting him to make a move on you, and now I guess he has."

"Yeah, it looks that way. The cops got there before we could take a closer look at those shooters, but I know they came from Nuncio. I don't know what's got his panties in a twist, but when he attacked me and my wife, he went too far."

From what Bolan had heard in the common room, Dominic's side had made the first moves, and Nuncio had been playing defense. But he didn't know the truth of it. To be honest, he didn't care.

He had shot those men on the street because they were shooting at him. He had no animosity toward them, or any loyalty to Chiarello. He was allied with Dominic only because he hadn't had a path directly to Nuncio, and he figured that one way or another, being in the middle of the fight would take him where he wanted to go.

It was about Ivory Wave. About Angela Fulton, and all the other Angela Fultons still at risk. Dominic Chiarello was nothing but a vehicle—one he would ride as long as he could until he reached his destination.

"Here's what we're going to do," Chiarello continued. "We're going after Nunce. No ambush bullshit, either. I know he's holed up in that building of his, downtown. We're going in there and we're not coming out again until my brother is dead. Nobody shoots at my wife. Not even him."

"Makes sense," Bolan said. "But attacking an office building in the middle of downtown? That's going to attract some attention."

Chiarello nodded. "That's right. But this is Friday night.

That's not a big nightlife part of town. Even when I lived here before, they rolled the sidewalks up there at six on Friday and didn't unroll them again until Monday morning. So we'll make our play tonight. The law's going to be on us pretty fast, so we've got to be faster. Get in, get Nunce and get out. Hopefully we'll be done by the time anybody hears the noise."

"You have anything like antitank ordnance?" Bolan asked. "We'll need it to get in fast."

"I got a line on some H&K GMGs," Chiarello said. "From the same source that supplied the submachine guns. But they haven't come through yet."

"I might be able to help with that," Bolan told him. "I have a couple of LAWs and an AT4."

Chiarello looked impressed. "Didn't you just fly in from Vegas? You can't check that shit with your bags."

"I believe in being prepared," Bolan said.

"The Boy Scouts never should've let you go."

"To tell you the truth, they were always a little tame for me."

"How much time you need, Kenner?"

Bolan calculated the distance to the airport and back. "Ninety minutes," he said. "And a ride."

"You got it. We're going in tonight, but not until midnight, when the streets in that neighborhood are completely deserted. That'll give you plenty of time to pick up the hardware, and then we'll meet up here and hammer out a plan."

"I've already got a plan, Mr. Chiarello."

Chiarello's left eyebrow arched. "You do?"

"We blow up the doors, go inside and shoot people," Bolan said. "You think it needs to be more complicated than that?"

Chiarello laughed. "I guess not. I think that'll about cover it."

22

Nuncio was sitting alone in his office, which had essentially become his home. He had set up a cot in one corner, and he had been clever enough to put a kitchen in the building when he had bought and converted it. It wasn't big enough to feed everybody, but he was the boss, and his needs came first. He was thinking about the only thing that had been on his mind lately—why his brother had it in for him, and what he could do about it. He hoped that was being taken care of right now.

Then someone knocked at his door, a hesitant *tap-tap-tap,* and he knew it hadn't been. "What?" he demanded.

The door opened and Gino came in, walking as if there might be land mines under the floor. Gino had never married, hadn't had many girlfriends, in fact. Physically, he was almost the opposite of his brother, slight and pale. Nuncio had wondered many times if his late wife had taken a lover or two, because it didn't seem that Gino could possibly be his son. He had also wondered if Gino was gay. He had tried to tell himself it wouldn't matter to him, but of course that was a lie. He would consider it a betrayal.

At the moment, however, it was the favored son, Massimo, who was the traitor. Nuncio thought there had to be a lesson in there somewhere, but he couldn't spare the time to try to figure it out. "What is it, Gino?"

"They missed Uncle Dom," he said.

"Who did?"

"The trap we set. You were right—Uncle Dom and Aunt Annamaria, they left the house and drove into the city. But the trap didn't work. Marco got a call from Joey B."

There were three guys on the payroll named Joey, all of them new, hitters brought in just for this fight. Fortunately they all had different last names, so they went by their initials."

"Did Joey B explain why he's a miserable fucking failure?"

"He didn't have time to. According to Marco, he was dying fast. The rest of them were dead, he said, or near enough."

"All of them?"

"That's what Joey said."

"And why didn't Marco bring me this news?"

"He's busy with something else, I guess. He asked me to tell you."

Nuncio sighed. "So the guy who's been with me the longest, who's one of my closest friends, even him I can't trust."

"You can trust Marco. And me."

"If Marco's busy with something, it's not something I told him to do," Nuncio said. "That means he's probably busy looking for a way out of this. Selling me out to Dom, maybe."

"He wouldn't!"

"He would, Gino. You got to be realistic here. We got some good guys on our side, guys who've made reputations all over the country. But for all we know, Dom's got an army. We're in here and he's out there. This would be the time to get out, if you wanted to go."

Gino looked as if he might burst into tears. That would be just the confidence builder Nuncio needed. "Papa! No way I'm leaving you! No fucking way!" he added, as if the swearword would make it more meaningful.

Nuncio swore, too. Probably too much. But some guys in the life, they had seen *GoodFellas* one time too many. Pesci could pull it off, but most guys just sounded like idiots when they tried. That was one reason Nuncio had tried to take his business interests legit, tried to raise his sons in a different environment than the one he and Dom had grown up in.

The other reason, of course, was that Dom had wound up inside. Dom was tough enough to take it, but Nuncio didn't think he was. If he had been looking at twenty-five years in a cage, he would have ended himself somehow. Dom had gone through it and come out stronger.

That was the key difference between them. That was why Dom would win this fight.

"Papa?" Gino asked.

"What?" Nuncio snapped. He'd had a moment of weakness, a moment of believing that he had already lost, and the kid had seen it. He had to do something.

"Are you okay?"

"I'm fine," Nuncio said. Even as the words slipped from his mouth, the idea came to him. "There's something you have to do for me, Gino."

"You know all you have to do is say the word."

"Where's Marco?"

"He's in his office." One flight down, Nuncio knew, with almost the same view. A little less lake, a little more of the building across the street.

"Perfect," Nuncio said. "You're carrying, right?"

Gino drew his jacket aside, showed his father the Glock 9 at his hip. Nuncio wasn't sure he had ever fired it, certainly not in anything like a life-or-death situation. "Of course."

"Go on downstairs. Kill him."

"Kill Marco?"

"That's what I said." Nuncio bit off the words, pissed off that the boy would even question a direct order.

"But—"

"He's turned against us," Nuncio said. "He's gotta go. And I shouldn't have to explain myself to you."

"You don't. But—"

"Again with the buts!" Nuncio slid his top desk drawer open. He had a piece under his armpit, but Gino knew he had one in the drawer, as well. When he spoke again, he had regained control of his temper. His voice was even, measured. Cold. "Take care of it, Gino."

"Yes, Papa," Gino said. No more arguing.

Good thing, too.

Nuncio had to have his only remaining son on his side. He could come out of this whole thing on top, he was sure. That momentary loss of confidence was a fluke, that was all. He would best Dom finally, and he would get back to his real interests—his businesses. Making bank.

He would crush Dom, and then the rest of this bullshit would blow over.

It wouldn't take long now.

As MIDNIGHT NEARED, a convoy of vehicles cruised down Rockwell Avenue, their headlights off. Streetlights provided all the illumination they needed, and there were few other vehicles on the road, and no pedestrians. Chiarello had been right about one thing—the place closed up tight on a Friday night.

They stopped a couple of blocks from the NDC building. The building across the street, the one with the restaurant where Bolan had eaten, blocked their view of it, and presumably the view of them from there. Men issued from the vehicles, and many of them gathered around the back of the Navigator that Bolan had been driving. He had been upgraded, thanks to Chiarello's word to Artie, from simple gunman to driver and armorer.

That last was also thanks to Stony Man, not that he would tell these people that.

Charlie Mott had included some heavy-duty firepower when he had made that delivery to Bolan. The soldier unzipped the heavy black bag he'd been carrying around and handed out two disposable M72 Light Antiarmor Weapons—LAWs. Rocket launchers, in short. They were old, but still functional.

Perhaps more useful, he had a considerably more modern AT4-CS. The CS stood for confined space, which meant the issue of back-blast, which had originally made the weapon iffy for use in urban conflicts, had been solved. A saltwater countermass absorbed the back blast; the spray that resulted was much less problematic than the fireball that had been a problem before. The muzzle velocity had been slightly reduced, but the trade-off was considered worth it for urban use. The weapon's big drawback was that it was built to be fired only once. But the AST warhead inside it would make that one use a worthy one.

"What the hell is that?" Massimo asked.

"Think of it as a key," Bolan said.

"A key?"

"You have a key to your dad's building?"

"Yes."

"You want to use it? Open the door and let us in?"

Massimo laughed. "They'd butcher me."

"Right," Bolan said. "That's why we'll use my key." He hoisted the weapon, showed Massimo the basics. He took off the safety pin, then moved the sight covers, causing the sights to pop into place. "This doesn't have a bad back-blast," he explained. "Compared to other models. But you still don't want to stand behind me when I use it."

"I'll be standing next to you," Massimo said. "I want to see that son of a bitch in action."

"Just not too close," Bolan said. He handed the weapon to Massimo while he inserted earplugs and pulled on a pair of goggles. A full helmet would have been better, but space and weight had both been issues.

"What does it shoot?" somebody asked.

Bolan tapped the olive-drab tube. "It's preloaded," he said, "with an antistructure tandem warhead. It carries two charges. The first one has a shallow penetration, but makes a big hole. The second goes through the hole and blows up anything or anybody on the inside. My key to the castle."

"That thing looks awesome," Massimo said.

"Let's find out. Wait a minute." He took a couple of minutes to explain firing the LAWs to the two men who had ended up with the weapons. Dominic Chiarello had come with them, and he stood around with his hands in his pockets, supervising but not taking part.

All in all, they could deal out some serious damage to Nuncio's home base before even getting inside. Of course, it would be a noisy entry. Once they got in, they'd have to move fast and get out.

Or Bolan would, anyway. He didn't care if the police rounded up the rest of them. It would be for the best, in fact.

But Bolan had a particular mission, and he wanted to get it done.

Once they were outfitted, nineteen men walked toward the NDC building. Bolan had the smaller of his zippered gear bags hanging against his hip, the strap cutting diagonally across his chest. He let Massimo carry the AT4, and he handled it as easily as a child's toy. He was grinning like an idiot. It was the first time Bolan had seen such a broad smile on the big man's face, and it gave him an idea.

"You want to fire it?" he asked.

"Really?"

"Sure. Nothing to it."

"Hell, yes!" Massimo replied.

"Okay. When we get into position I'll show you the steps."

"Cool!"

For a hardened killer, Massimo's enthusiasm was boyish. Bolan figured the reason for that enthusiasm was the fact that he had just been handed a device that would make killing easier than ever. Whatever the source, he intended to take advantage of it. He moved a little closer to Massimo as they walked, and spoke with his voice low.

"You probably know a lot about your father's business, don't you?" he asked, handing over the eyewear and earplugs.

"Sure, I guess."

"Tell you what—we've been thinking about getting into that bath salts business. Ivory Wave, and all that. How's that going for you?"

"Great!" Massimo said. "Papa says it's better than cocaine in the eighties. Low overhead, high margin, customers can't get enough of it. And we don't need to worry about anybody going to jail, because the drugs we lace it with are hard to detect, so you're not having to hire kids to sell it on street corners or anything like that. Or paying lawyers and bail costs. It's probably our single most profitable sector."

"Wow," Bolan said. "Now I'm sorry we didn't dive in sooner. Whose idea was it for you guys, originally? Somebody took home a nice bonus, I'm guessing."

"Oh, that was all Papa. He heard about it someplace, you know, and said we should try it out. Gino and I, we weren't so sure. But then, we weren't involved back in the eighties when coke was booming, so we didn't know. Turns out, if you sell something that gets people hooked, you've got a nice steady revenue stream. Our chemist was able to twist ours and make it better and even more addictive, so our numbers are almost double anyone else's."

"So it's addictive, this stuff?"

"Oh, hell yes. Don't ever try it, that's what I hear. But sell it like crazy, because people who do try it keep on wanting more."

"Well, I don't know about you," Bolan said, "but I'm addicted to revenue streams. Thanks for the tip."

"Hey, no problem, dude."

They reached the diner on the corner, and Bolan held up a hand to stop the procession. He waited until Dominic Chiarello joined him at the corner. It was the old man's show theoretically, even though he had ceded the tactical decisions to Bolan. Still, he needed to look as if he was involved. Bolan caught his eye and Chiarello gave him a nod.

"When we get around the corner, they'll know we're here," Bolan said. His voice was a low rumble, but he knew everybody could hear him. "So we're going to have to set up fast. Our initial volley is going to make a lot of noise, and it's going to let anybody in that building—anybody within a mile of here—know that we're out here." He pointed out positions for the LAWs, and Massimo and the AT4. He wanted the AT4 to take out the front door, the LAWs on the garage gate and the gunmen watching it. He positioned men with MP5s and high-capacity magazines aiming at the windows facing the lake.

"Fire until you're empty," he said. "Then come back over here and reposition. When vehicles come out of the garage, take them out." He indicated four men. "You guys go into the garage when we blow the gate. Anybody who's already in a vehicle and moving toward the exit, you can let them go unless you need to defend yourself. Massimo, how many staircases inside feed into the garage?"

"Just one," Massimo said. "And the elevator."

"And how many staircases on the inside?"

"One from the lobby up to the mezzanine," Massimo replied. "Two internal ones, including the one to the garage."

"Okay, two of you stay by the elevator doors and punch the button. When it arrives, kill anybody inside and disable it. You might be able to just leave a body between the doors. They'll bump against it, but it won't go anywhere as long as the doors can't close. If you come up with a better way, though, do that. The other two, come up the stairs and shoot anybody coming down.

"The rest of us will go in through the front doors, or the hole that AT4's going to make there. When you hit the stairs, don't turn around and head back down or you'll be shot by our own guys coming up. Four guys peel off at each floor—two from each interior staircase. Get inside the doors and start shooting. Careful you're not shooting at each other from opposite ends of the hall. We're going for maximum casualty count here. Everybody okay with that?"

A few men nodded. Nobody objected. Bolan knew the plan was rudimentary at best, and would get a lot of his men killed.

That didn't matter, though. They weren't really his men. They were murderers, every one of them, and the country would be a better place without them.

He turned to Chiarello. "Maybe you should stay here until we've cleared the building and taken Nuncio. Then you can come in and assume control of the operation."

"As long as my brother's alive," Chiarello said. "That's the main thing. Save him for me to deal with."

"Everybody got that?" Bolan asked. "He'll probably be on the top floor, hiding under something. Leave him to me, and let me know when the lower floors are cleared."

More nods and grunts of assent came his way. The men were anxious to get going, their adrenaline revving up their nervous systems. If they didn't get into action soon, they'd be jumpy, worthless.

"Okay, then. Any last questions?"

None came.

"On my mark," Bolan said. "Heavy ordnance first, then

we move out." He watched them all to make sure they were ready, then counted down.

On his word, the men bearing the LAWs and large-capacity MP5s fanned out to the spots he had indicated. Massimo stepped forward with his AT4, and Bolan made sure no one was behind him.

Once the men were set, Bolan shouted out, "Fire!" and the street exploded into booming noises, then explosions as the rounds hit home. The rocket sailed across the street, hit right next to the big bronze doors, blew, and then as expected, the secondary charge continued through the hole and exploded on the inside. Anybody standing near it would have been torn to shreds and blown up against whatever walls remained.

The LAW rockets took down the garage gate and part of the wall. One of the gunmen on the inside ran out into the street, half his face sheared away. A quick triburst from an SMG finished him.

The MP5 rounds crashed through windows and pelted anybody trying to see what was coming. When the barrage was over, men raced to cover.

Then the real attack began, with Bolan leading the way. Nuncio's men were shooting from the few windows that had an angle toward the intersection, but for the most part, when Bolan had brought the window gunners back in from their original positions, he had removed most of their potential targets. The side facing the diner, above the garage entrance, was a solid, blank slab. The greatest danger would be when he led men in through the front door, which would take them directly beneath the windows. Then Nuncio's guys could fire straight down at them. If they met any resistance at the point of entry, it could get ugly.

The group split up as they crossed the street, the smaller force heading toward the gaping garage entrance. Bolan took the rest close to the building, and they hugged stone as they worked toward the doorway. They had successfully cleared most of the windows. A few shots came from the farthest one, but the angle was bad and the rounds impacted harmlessly against the street.

The AT4 had obliterated the left-hand door and a large chunk of the wall beside it. Bolan flattened against the wall for an instant, then spun into the opening, weapon at the ready, and scanned the visible interior. There was a large lobby area, marble-floored, detailed in rich wood and brass. But the floor had a crater in it, and body parts littered the rest. Scorch marks spread out around the blast area, and blood was everywhere, trails of it like lines on a road map, linking human tissue and debris and dropped weaponry.

Bolan stepped inside.

The lobby's ceiling soared overhead, two stories high, with a graceful staircase sweeping up to the mezzanine. The only pieces of furniture on the ground floor were a reception-security counter with some video monitors behind it, and a waiting area with couches and chairs. A huge cut-crystal chandelier was suspended from the ceiling, and Bolan saw trace amounts of blood on the lower rows, twenty feet above the floor. The smell of smoke and raw flesh warred for supremacy in the air.

Not a living soul was in sight.

That wouldn't last, Bolan knew. By now, they knew the building had been breached. Whoever was still alive on the upper floors was preparing some kind of defense. So far, Dominic's men had made it through with no casualties, but that was about to change.

From this point forward, blood would be spilled on both sides.

23

Gino had taken the elevator down, his knees too weak to trust on the stairs.

He had never killed before. His brother had, he knew. Once, at least, that he was aware of. Massimo had always had a violent streak, though, even when they were kids. Massimo had been a scrapper, then he had grown huge, seemingly overnight, and become notorious as a bully. When their father had announced that he was adopting the straight-and-narrow path, Gino thought sure Massimo would object to their old man throwing away his chance to be one of those Mob legends, like the Iceman or Tommy Pitera. Maybe he was wrong, maybe there was a decent core somewhere inside his brother. But if there was, he hid it well.

More than likely, he had killed again. He had always struck Gino as a killer waiting for his chance to shine.

That urge had never run strong in Gino, though. He had been relieved at their father's decision. The straight life was the safe life, without prison worries or fears that one day he'd turn the key to start his car and ignite a bomb, or turn the wrong corner and find a man with a gun waiting for him.

Now, simply by getting out of prison, his uncle seemed to have changed all that.

On legs that threatened to give way with every step, he walked past the NDC executive offices, his own included, as well as the empty one that his uncle Dom had never used, to get to Marco's. It was a corner office, next to the one Gordon Hawkins used and directly below his father's, though only half the size. Marco's responsibilities with the company were limited; mostly he was there as a sounding board for the old man, a crucial voice of reason.

Gino had always loved Marco, who was more of an uncle to him than Dom had ever been. Dom had done much for Massimo, but every time he saw Gino, he looked at him as if he was a stranger and a bit of a pest.

He stopped at Marco Cosimo's door. It was open, but he knocked anyway. The man was sitting at his desk, staring at the window as if important messages were being beamed to him from the distant lake. At Gino's knock, Cosimo swiveled in his chair. "Gino," he said.

"Something outside?" Gino asked. He held the Glock behind his back.

"No. I don't know. I thought I heard…I don't know what. Probably just a car going by. What are you—"

He didn't answer, and Gino never brought the pistol around, because from outside the window, flashes came, bright as daylight, and with them came thunder like the hoofbeats of the Four Horsemen. "Fuck," Cosimo said when the building started to rock, and Gino forgot all about the task at hand.

THROUGH A DOORWAY behind the reception counter was the internal stairway that led down into the garage and up into the bowels of the building. Bolan sent six men up those stairs, to be joined at some point by the two coming up from the garage. He led the remaining nine, which included Massimo and Nico, up the grand staircase. Artie D'Amato had stayed behind with Chiarello.

"Remember the drill," he said. "Up here we'll probably find some resistance, as well as another staircase leading up.

Finish off everybody on this floor, then go up and a couple of you peel off on each floor. When you've cleared one, move up to the next. I'll head up to the top and see if I can find Nuncio, then work down until I find you again."

At the top of the stairs he stopped, crouched low and showed the barrel of his MP5 before he showed his head. Nobody shot at either one. He peered over the uppermost stair. The mezzanine had a kind of loft-balcony area where people could sit and look out over the lobby, but from the untrammeled thickness of the carpeting it didn't look as if it got a lot of use.

Past that were a pair of frosted glass doors. Bolan guessed there were conference rooms behind those, but since he could smell a faint aroma of cooked food and stale coffee, it was also possible that there was a kitchen or lunchroom or even some offices. He couldn't see any motion through the glass, but they were mostly opaque.

One thing was certain, though—when he approached them, he would have the chandelier at his back, an easy target.

Bolan paused, unzipped the leather bag against his hip and withdrew a grenade. "Massimo," he whispered, "go over there beside the door and yank it open on my count."

Massimo moved immediately, keeping to the side of the glass so he wouldn't be silhouetted against it. He waited for Bolan to count down with his fingers, the soldier pulling the pin with his teeth as he did. On one, Massimo grabbed the big steel handle and pulled the door open. Gunfire came from inside, shattering the glass but soaring over the heads of the men on the stairs. As soon as the doors were parted, Bolan threw the grenade.

It hit, bounced, rolled.

Then it blew.

When it did, Bolan charged, strafing the far side of the

doors with 9 mm rounds from his MP5. Massimo spun around the ruined doors and joined him, and others followed.

Through the doors they found a short corridor, with a glass-walled conference room on one side and a couple of doorways beyond that. Two guys were in the conference room, one lying next to the long table with a sixteen-inch shard of glass from the wall embedded in his upper chest, another slumped against a wall with blood running from his nose, mouth and ears. Bolan and Massimo went to the first door, flanked it, then entered, Bolan going low and Massimo high. It was, as he had thought, a kitchen. A couple of guys had taken refuge inside, and they fired semiautomatic pistols from behind a refrigerator and a tipped-over table. One round thunked into the doorjamb, showering Massimo with splinters, and another missed entirely and cored into the wall.

Both men returned fire with quick bursts from the SMGs. Bolan's tore through the tabletop, and the guy behind it flailed his arms as he flopped backward, a rooster tail of blood spraying from his skull. Massimo destroyed the fridge and the man using it for cover.

Bolan's gun clicked on an empty chamber. He ejected the magazine, slammed home a new one and tossed aside the spent. He could hear gunfire in other parts of the building now, a constant presence.

Other men had cleared the room behind the second doorway, which Bolan saw as he passed contained vending machines, a TV and more tables and chairs. Beyond that the hallway ended in a T-shaped niche, with an elevator on one side and a stairwell door opposite. The other stairwell was on the far side of the building, not accessible from the mezzanine level, so this was the one that no one had ventured into yet.

The soldier yanked open the door and waved some of his men through. Gunfire rang out from above, echoing down the stairs, and one of the men fell right away as machine-

gun fire cut stitches down his torso. The second one tried to
reverse course, but a round caught him in the thigh. His leg
buckled and then more slugs hammered into him. He danced
on the floor, like a marionette worked by a spastic puppeteer,
until death took him.

Bolan ducked into the staircase and sprayed lead upward.
He was joined by Massimo and another guy Bolan recognized as Micelli. A cry came from above, and a body went
over the rail, dropped to their level and landed in a heap. An
answering burst came from somewhere overhead, but the men
moved forward, finding better angles, and fired again. This
time a gun clattered down the stairs, followed by the sound
of a person sliding down.

The Executioner took the lead, going up, stepping over
the weapon. When he reached the man on the stairs, he saw
the guy was clutching another little .38 revolver in quivering
hands. Blood was bubbling over his lips and his eyelids were
fluttering. He was as good as dead, but a reflexive contrac-
tion could still injure or kill one of Bolan's men. He started to
raise his gun, to administer a *coup de grâce*, then decided he
wouldn't waste a bullet. He passed the man and continued on.

At the next landing was a heavy steel door with a "3" sten-
ciled on it. When other men arrived on the landing, Bolan
drew it open and waved a couple inside. The rest saw what he
had done, and they knew their orders. Bolan ran on up, passing the next couple of doors, his mind on his ultimate target.

24

Marco Cosimo turned away from the window and saw Gino standing there with the Glock in his hands. For an instant his skin went pale, but then he nodded. "Good idea," he said, crossing to a wardrobe standing against one wall. "Sounds like we'll need that, and then some." He took a pump-action shotgun from the cabinet, a wicked-looking thing, matte-black and sinister. He pumped a shell into the chamber and handed the weapon to Gino, who tucked the Glock back into its holster. Marco got out a second shotgun, for himself.

"There was a time," Cosimo said, "that I would have killed for your father, or died for him. But he wanted to turn his back on that life, on that ethic. So you know what? Fuck him. Whatever doom is out there, he brought down on himself. I'll kill anyone who gets in my way, but I'll be damned if I'm dying for him. If you're smart, you'll do the same. Get out of this building and never look back."

Cosimo started for the doorway. When Gino spoke, he could barely find his voice; the first word came out as an awkward squeak. "Mr. Cosimo, what'd you say about my father?"

Cosimo stopped at the door and began to turn back toward Gino. "I said, fuck h—"

Gino pulled the trigger. From less than six feet away, the shotgun's blast ripped through the older man's midsection and blew out as a thick red mist from his back. Gino looked away, trying to rush from the office without seeing any more than he just had or stepping in the stringy mess on the floor. He threw the shotgun away from him and burst through the door just as Gordon Hawkins reached it. "Gino?"

"He's dead," Gino said. "Marco. I—"

He was about to explain when three men came in from the stairwell. He had seen one of them before—a tall, skinny guy with a black crewcut, one of Artie D'Amato's thugs. The other two were new to him.

Hawkins swore, and Gino realized he should draw the Glock at the same instant that all three men pulled their triggers, and it was the last thought either of them ever had.

BOLAN PAUSED FOR a three-count behind the steel door with the white "6" on it, letting his heartbeat and breathing steady after the dash up the stairs. He heard gunfire from what seemed like every floor but this one. He didn't for a moment believe that this floor would be undefended, but he had wanted to come up alone because from this point forward, his mission was different from everybody else's. He'd needed them only to help him get into the building, but now they would just be in the way.

He eased the door open a crack and peered through. Nobody in sight. Across the hall was the elevator, its door closed; presumably it was trapped in the garage, though he had no way of knowing for sure that had happened. He opened the door wider and slipped through.

At the corner, he stayed close to the wall and slid his Tanto combat knife from its ballistic nylon sheath. He crouched low and held the knife so its blade protruded past the wall, checking the image reflected in the steel. It was no mirror, but it was good enough. He didn't see any movement, or anything that looked human. Still at a crouch, he moved so that just enough of his head showed past the wall to see with his right eye.

Three doors down the right side of the hallway, one on the left. The hall was short and ended in a spacious area, kind of a cul-de-sac, with a reception desk in its center. Bolan judged that there would be one more door there, to the left but out of sight from here, and it would lead to an office that commanded the best views from the building, out toward Lake Erie. That—unless he had already fled—was where Bolan expected to find Nuncio Chiarello.

Four doors to get past first.

They would know he was here when the first shot was fired, so the element of surprise wouldn't serve him for long. He reached into his zippered bag and pulled out the last grenade, this one an M-18 smoke canister. Better than nothing. He pulled the pin and hurled the canister down the hall. It landed with a thunk and rolled toward the open area, thick smoke billowing from its emission holes.

From at least two of the doorways—through the smoke, Bolan couldn't be certain of the number—people fired automatic weapons into the hall, wasting ammunition on a grenade instead of spotting their target.

It didn't tell him much, but it confirmed his suspicion.

He stayed put a few seconds longer, waiting. Sure enough, a man came to one of the doorways and stepped out, looking first in the direction the grenade had rolled, then turning to see where it had come from.

Bolan didn't let him finish the turn.

He fired a short burst from the MP5, catching the man center mass, picking him up off the floor briefly and then dropping him with a liquid slapping sound.

More rounds flew into the hallway, pocking the walls. This time Bolan was able to isolate which doors they had come from. Two on the right and the one on the left. The doors were staggered slightly, so no one could look into an office from the one across the hall.

Still, soldiers who knew what they were doing could catch him in a cross fire as he tried to pass. Some on this floor had displayed an amateurish eagerness to pull their triggers, but he couldn't count on that continuing. Nuncio could have hired people with just as much experience as the ones Dominic had found.

Bolan had no more grenades, and his last magazine was already in the MP5. Once that was done, he was down to the Desert Eagle on his belt and the Beretta 93-R under his arm, and of course the combat knife.

He decided speed was his best ally, aided by the smoke to mask his movements. The soldier broke into a sprint, racing past the first door. At the second he caught a glimpse of movement and opened up with the MP5, blasting whatever had moved into the wallpaper. By the time he reached the third, rounds were streaking out the door and across the hall, chest high, so he hit the ground and slid like a desperate ballplayer trying for an extra base, firing through the doorway until the magazine was empty.

And then someone swung out the last door holding a Striker-12, the shotgun known as the street sweeper, with its 12-round capacity.

Bolan was still on the ground, rolling to his feet. He came up out of his crouch ready to throw the empty SMG, then to cover the distance between him and the gunman and engage him in hand-to-hand. But he heard the flat crack of a pistol, and the front of the shotgun-wielder's head exploded. He tumbled toward Bolan, revealing a man standing behind him holding a Beretta 92A1. The newcomer looked young, but partly that was due to his unkempt red hair and the spray of freckles across his nose.

"I was told to expect the unexpected," he said. "I guess you're it."

"You must be the Fed I heard about," Bolan replied. "Guess you're in pretty deep. Sorry if I'm spoiling anything."

"Don't worry about it," the agent said. "The more of them you take out, the fewer times I'll have to testify in court. I've already got plenty of detail to put in my report, so it's all good."

"The one I'm looking for is Nuncio Chiarello."

The agent jerked a thumb over his left shoulder, indicating the open area. "The big office," he said. "Help yourself. I'm gonna go see if there's anybody left to arrest on the fifth floor. I wouldn't mind seeing Marco Cosimo in a cell."

He headed for the stairs. Bolan drew his Desert Eagle, and as he stepped into the open circular area, one more assailant showed himself. He had been hiding behind the reception desk with a 9 mm handgun. He appeared confident, aiming with a steady hand, showing little of his head while he did. Bolan dropped, a sudden, surprising move that left him flat on the floor with his arms extended before him. The man behind the desk rose slightly to see where his target had gone, which was when Bolan fired two shots in quick succession. The .44-caliber slugs sheared off the left quarter of the man's skull, and he fell across the reception desk, blood gushing from the wound.

The last door was exactly where Bolan had expected it to be. It was a solid oak door, closed and locked. Since the only other way in was through the windows, six stories above the ground and with no ledge—and Bolan with no climbing gear—he fired a couple of shots into the locking mechanism, then kicked the door right beside the knob. Wood chips flew and the door swung open.

The office could have been an emperor's suite, with fine artwork, expensive rugs and rich-looking furnishings. But the emperor sat in his desk chair, seeming very small and alone. Nuncio Chiarello looked even older than his older brother

Dominic. His hair was white and fine, his neck wattled, the skin on his face appearing to be paper-thin, with blue tracery of veins beneath it. His hands were mottled, knuckles enlarged, fingers slender and trembling. A .45 automatic lay on the desk before him, but he made no move toward it.

"You're Nuncio," Bolan said. It wasn't a question.

"Yes."

"I've been looking for you."

"I've been right here."

"I only had one piece of information at a time. But the trail eventually led straight to you."

"What trail is that?" Nuncio asked.

"One made of phony bath salts and littered with the bodies of children. A trail of Ivory Wave."

Nuncio made a dismissive gesture with his right hand. "Spare me the cheap moralizing. How many did you kill to get in here?"

"Fair point," Bolan said. "I never claimed to be pure. But the ones I killed were killers themselves, or they were trying to kill me. Or both."

"I'm no killer," Nuncio said. "I turned my back on that path years ago. I'm a businessman, like any other."

"You're the worst kind of killer," Bolan countered. "The way I heard it, you did all your face-to-face killing when you were a young man. Then you decided there was greater profit to be earned by killing people you would never see, and from a distance. We know the secrets in Ivory Wave now. I'm going to put the whole thing out of business for good."

Nuncio sneered at him. "You're crazy!"

"Are you going to deny running the Ivory Wave business in the Midwest?"

"No! Okay? That what you wanted to hear? I guess you'll do whatever you're going to do, no matter what I say. So do it, already."

"Your son told me it was your baby, start to finish. You learned about the stuff and saw the potential, so you set up a factory and built a distribution network."

"I'm a capitalist. You got something against that?" Nuncio asked.

"Only when your product is poison."

"How's that saying go? One man's poison…"

"'One man's meat is another man's poison,'" Bolan quoted, walking deeper into the large office. "I don't think that applies here."

"What do we do now?" Nuncio asked. "You going to talk me to death?"

"I just needed to hear you say it," Bolan told him. He crossed to the big windows and looked out at the buildings standing between here and the waterfront. Moonlight glimmered on the surface of the lake. "Now I have to decide whether to kill you or turn you over to the FBI agent who's been infiltrating your operation."

He had to wait two or three seconds longer than he had expected before he heard the rustle of fabric from the desk, the clunk of the gun being snatched up. When he did, he whirled and fired the Desert Eagle, all in the same motion. Nuncio stared at him, his surprise amplified by the third eye between and slightly above his first two. Blood trickled from it. The gun fell from limp fingers, and then Nuncio began a slow-motion slide from his desk chair.

Bolan holstered his weapon and started for the door, only to see Massimo step in front of it, blocking his exit. "You killed him," Massimo said.

"Isn't that what this was all about?"

"Not for you. I heard what you said. At the end, there."

"I didn't start this war," Bolan said. "But I'm happy to finish it."

"He's my father," Massimo said. His voice was strangely flat, free of any emotion at all.

"That's right." His task done, Bolan was suddenly conscious of the passage of time. By now the Cleveland police had to be on their way, maybe with full riot gear. Big-city police forces these days fielded tactical squads almost military in their training and equipment. He put his right hand against the plane of the big man's chest, giving him a gentle shove. "If it wasn't me, your uncle would have done it. You knew he wouldn't survive this. Let's go, Massimo."

As experienced as Bolan was, Massimo's move surprised him. He grabbed Bolan's wrist with his huge hands and bent it backward, at the same time driving his forehead forward to smash into Bolan's face. The Executioner managed to turn his head in time to take the brunt of the blow on his cheek, saving his nose from certain breakage. Still, the impact blinded him momentarily. He tried to wrench his hand free, but Massimo gripped it with his left, using his right to shoot two powerful jabs into Bolan's midsection.

Bolan got a hard left into Massimo's jaw, staggering the big man, and allowing him to wrench his right arm from the giant's grip before it was snapped. He punched once with his right, but on impact pain lanced through it, all the way to the shoulder. Massimo returned the favor, his huge fists hard and punishing.

Shaking off the pain, Bolan tried to sweep Massimo's legs out from under him in an effort to get past the doorway. But Massimo's legs were like tree trunks, his feet well spaced, his stance solid. He kept his left leg extended just enough that from his angle, Bolan couldn't get to his groin. He aimed a snap kick at Massimo's left leg, just below the knee. Massimo anticipated it, shifting just enough that the kick dealt only a glancing blow.

Moving quickly, Massimo waded inside Bolan's reach, negating the strength the soldier could put into any given punch. The big man was unstoppable, driving Bolan backward struggling for balance. Finally Bolan tried to step aside, to clear himself of Massimo's bulk long enough to launch an effective attack, but the young killer swung both arms around like a baseball bat, catching him just as one foot left the ground. The collision knocked Bolan sideways, slamming him hard against Nuncio's desk.

It hurt, but it gave Bolan the instant he needed. He snatched the heavy stone lighter off the desk and fired it at Massimo, who raised a hand to block it but missed. The lighter hit him on the left side of his face and bounced away. Massimo cried out, and Bolan charged. He rained hard shots to the same cheek, a right-left-right combination that made the big man take three steps back and turn his head away.

Bolan's hands came back bloody. He was reaching for the Beretta to finish this when Massimo lunged again. As he did, the Executioner saw a flap of skin hanging loosely from his cheekbone, the white of bone and muscle showing beneath it. Blood painted his cheek and chin, spattering his jacket. Bolan took an off-balance shot to his left shoulder, but he paid Massimo back by slamming the butt of his palm into his adversary's ruined cheek.

Massimo roared in pain and hooked his left arm around Bolan's neck, drawing him into a bear hug and punishing his opponent with a series of rights. Bolan raised his booted foot high and brought it down hard and fast on Massimo's instep. He felt bones collapse under the weight, and Massimo's arms went slack.

Still, the big man wouldn't go down, but the tide had turned. Bolan danced around him, lashing out with fists and feet, returning often to the gaping wound at Massimo's cheek. That eye was already swelling, half shut and more. Massimo was bleeding from a dozen other wounds: a broken nose, pulped lips, a gash that split his right eyebrow. He had slowed, but every now and then he landed a powerful fist, and Bolan knew he wouldn't want to look in a mirror anytime soon.

Finally Massimo caught him again, one of those big hands clutching Bolan's throat and pulling him close. Massimo's breath was hot in his face, tasting of blood and rage. His teeth snapped an inch from Bolan's nose, and the more the soldier struggled, the closer he drew it.

Bolan returned to what had worked before, stomping down on the same crushed instep. This time Massimo cried out and his grip slackened. Bolan got an elbow up and smashed it into Massimo's windpipe. For several more seconds the young killer stood gasping for breath, his hands clawing weakly at nothing, and then he pitched forward like a great redwood brought low by a lumberman's ax.

The Executioner watched him for a moment, collecting himself, catching his breath. Massimo twitched and writhed, but with less potency every instant. Bolan drew his Desert Eagle again and left him on the floor of his father's office. He might live and he might die, but either way, he would do it on his own terms, without Bolan as a witness.

Epilogue

Bolan encountered no resistance as he descended the stairwell that led to the garage. At the bottom, the two men assigned to wait there raised weapons when he reached the door, but recognized him and lowered their guns. He tossed them a cursory nod and hurried up the exit ramp. When he got to the SUV he had driven, he started to open the driver's door, but the sound of approaching sirens—from every direction—changed his plan. Instead, he went to the back, tossed the keys inside, removed the zippered bag and struck off on foot. He kept up a brisk pace until he reached the waterfront, then he slowed. Finding a bench, he sat and gazed out at the lake, watching the moon's reflection shimmy in the chop of the surf. He knew the police would take care of the Mob survivors. His part was over.

After a while he took out his phone and dialed a number. A woman answered, her voice thick with sleep.

"Gloria," he said, "is Eddie available?"

"No, he's—oh, it's you," she said. "I'm sorry, Matt. Since… you know, Angela, he's been sleeping so poorly, the doctor gave him a prescription. The pills really knock him out cold."

"I understand," Bolan said. "I thought he'd want to know— you both would. Sometimes it's hard to find justice in this world, and I don't know that I'd call it that anyway. But the pipeline—the one that Angela wound up on the end of—it's closed."

"It is?"

"I can't say another one won't open up sometime. But that one's shut down for good. The people who ran it won't run anything, ever again. That's the best I can do."

Gloria's voice sounded unutterably sad when she answered. "It's not enough, Matt, but nothing could be, ever. That's not your fault, though, and I know you can't work miracles. Still, you've done more than we could have asked. I thank you, and I know Eddie will, too, when he hears. You can't know how much this means to us."

After the call, Bolan sat on the bench awhile longer. A boat chugged across the lake, parallel to the shore, lights along its starboard side and in its wheelhouse making it look like a constellation fallen to earth.

It wasn't a miracle, just human beings setting out for a hard day's work.

But it would do.

* * * * *

Don Pendleton's Mack Bolan

LETHAL STAKES

A relentless enemy kills for a stake in a revolutionary missile system...

An Israeli defense contractor has constructed components for the Valkyrie missile — the closest thing to divine power the world has ever seen. Rogue elements are prepared to kill to control it, and the murder trail leads Bolan to uncover the conspiracy of a wealthy Chinese spymaster whose ultimate goal is to buy out the safety of the free world. The Executioner must hunt down a mastermind with unlimited resources and the ruthlessness to hijack world peace.

Available in July wherever books are sold.